FANTASTICAL CHRSITMAS COMPLETE COLLECTION

CONNOR WHITELEY

No part of this book may be reproduced in any form or by any electronic or mechanical means. Including information storage, and retrieval systems, without written permission from the author except for the use of brief quotations in a book review.

This book is NOT legal, professional, medical, financial or any type of official advice.

Any questions about the book, rights licensing, or to contact the author, please email connorwhiteley@connorwhiteley.net

Copyright © 2023 CONNOR WHITELEY

All rights reserved.

DEDICATION
Thank you to all my readers without you I couldn't do what I love.

AUTHOR OF THE FIREHEART FANTASY SERIES

CONNOR WHITELEY

MAGIC THAT BINDS

A HOLIDAY CONTEMPORARY FANTASY SHORT STORY

INTRODUCTION

Mood/ Genre: Light Contemporary Fantasy

Today's holiday short story is another one that is rather different compared to what I normally write, but in a good way of course.

There isn't really too much I can say about this light fantasy story, because the story really does speak for itself.

However, what I can say is today is what's known as Make A Gift day, so I immediately jumped to the fantasy genre to create a story inspired by the spirit of this made-up holiday.

So please check out this wonderful fantasy story about freedom, magic and gift-giving.

Enjoy!

MAGIC THAT BINDS

It might have started off as a hobby but to Janet making gifts was all part of the holiday season experience. It was amazing, wonderful to make people such wondrous gifts, Janet was known to everyone in Kent, England as the best gift maker because of her ability to infuse even the most hideous objects with her magic and make them stunning.

Janet stood in a smaller isle in a massive craft superstore surrounded by rows upon rows of beads in all their different sizes, textures and colours.

Beads might have been awful, small and annoying to some people, but to Janet they were magical things that were the best material to make gifts from. Their small round size meant it didn't take much magic to manipulate them into whatever shape she wanted.

And as a part-time teacher at the local sixth form for young magic users, the beads were perfect to allow them to experiment with their magic.

She had stopped using wooden and other large material a long time ago, young inexperienced magic users definitely shouldn't unleash the magical energy needed to manipulate large pieces of wood until they were ready.

Janet hated to think about all the fires, explosions and other accidents caused by them.

But beads were perfect.

The smell of the little plastic beads wasn't the best but when mixed together with flowers, natural materials and maybe even a hint of lavender, these beads would smell amazing, and that was what Janet loved about gift making.

The sound of other customers and their children in the other isles reminded Janet of her own love of the different crafts. She loved the bright lively strokes of painting and the wonderful hands-on nature of pottery.

But the containers of bright red, blue and green beads in front of her head were what Janet needed at this point in time. Maybe she could check out the paints and pottery bits later. Perhaps even her husband could buy her a few pieces for Christmas.

Janet placed her hands into the containers of the plastic beads. Their icy coldness felt amazing, their smooth cold texture was a stunning, beautiful contrast to her aged rough hands.

But she needed to find magic sensitive beads.

These types of beads were often made by magic users in the factories and mixed in with the rest of the beads to stop them from being detected (Not everyone was as respectable towards magic users as they should have been), but Janet had detected a strong number of the magical beads in this aisle alone.

That was unusual yet that was the last thing on Janet's priorities at the moment as her annoying (but wonderfully rich) client had given her an awful deadline to make a gift by the end of the day.

Janet didn't like to rush gifts. Each one was carefully planned, made and delivered. Each one took at least three days to make so making a wonderful gift in a single day was going to be difficult. Not impossible. Just difficult.

The only solace Janet could take from the impossible request was the amazing contract and payday that came with it. Ten thousand pounds for the gift and the exclusive contract of being the client's personal gift maker.

Normally that wouldn't interest Janet, but considering the client was a rich businessman who entertained hundreds of clients every year in London. The pay checks would be like shooting fish in a barrel.

Janet finished searching the containers in front of her head and frowned.

This was silly. She had detected the magic here and now they were gone. She was running out of time. Janet had to create this gift in time.

Janet closed her eyes and called on her powers, she used them to sense and search through the containers, if the beads were here then her magic should be able to find them.

Nothing. Except the moderately strong remains of their magical signatures.

Janet hated that the beads had been so close but she was too late to get them. Perhaps she could go and search the store and maybe the car park, then buy them off the person who had them, but Janet wasn't sure in the slightest.

"Mrs Janet Oblong?" an elderly lady said.

Janet looked at the tall elderly lady with her purple power suit, long brown hair and perfectly aged face. Janet couldn't understand how the woman could sound like a ninety-year-old but look not a day over thirty.

Well, she could. The woman had to be a fellow magic user.

"How do you know my name?" Janet asked.

The woman smiled. "I am Lady Michelle, and I know a lot about you,"

Janet didn't believe her in the slightest.

"Janet Oblong grew up in Canterbury England and went to university at The University of Magic in the city for five years, completing a degree in Psychology specialising in Magical Mental Health and then doing another degree in Magical Studies,"

Janet was impressed but surely this woman could have found all that out online. Maybe this Lady was a creepy stalker or something.

"I'm not a stalker, Janet,"

Janet's eyes widened.

"And before you think it, I am a telepath. That is my main discipline. My husband Lord Michelle is a lot better at it but I manage,"

Janet wanted to wonder who the hell this woman was, but she didn't, she couldn't have this Lady Michelle reading her thoughts. So she fell back on her training and what her degree had taught her to do.

Simply don't think about anything important.

"Clever Janet. I wasn't sure if you remembered your training,"

Janet stepped forward. "Do I know you?"

"In a way. I always watched your classes. Loved University myself. But I was always at the edges of everyone's mind,"

Janet took a step back. "Who the hell are you?"

"You seek beads to make a gift. I have beads and want a gift,"

Janet didn't even care if the woman read her mind anymore. This was just strange and crazy, the Lady Michelle was clearly a stalker of some kind. It wasn't natural for a telepath or any magic user to watch university students and read the thoughts at the edge of their minds.

It was probably the weirdest thing Janet had ever heard of.

"Oh now Janet, I have heard of stranger things. Me brushing past the edges of your mind isn't strange. It's comforting. I'm a guardian of sorts,"

Janet just wanted those beads and to go home.

She didn't have time for this Lady Michelle, or whatever the hell she was.

"A Guardian?" Janet asked, her voice unsure.

"Yes dear Janet. I used to work for the University's Mental Health Services and I spent my day brushing through the minds of the students checking on their wellbeing,"

"You're lying. You didn't check on their wellbeing. You invaded their privacy, and doesn't magical law prohibit you searching the minds of others?"

Lady Michelle laughed hard. "Dearest Janet, the Law is old and outdated. I might have scarred myself by looking through the thoughts of the students, and believe me it's... interesting what some people get up to. But I saved lives,"

Janet realised this woman certainly wasn't normal, but she felt like a woman with a purpose. This was no chance meeting or simply seeing Janet and wanting to talk. Lady Michelle had planned to meet her and make Janet talk to her.

"My client's your husband, isn't he?" Janet asked.

Lady Michelle nodded. "Clever girl. Sure, my husband doesn't know I am here but still. He wants the gift for me and I want something from you in return,"

"What?" Janet asked, checking for the nearest escape route.

"I want you to work for me,"

Janet's eyes narrowed. "Work for you? I don't

even know what you do,"

A family of small children and two parents walked into the aisle and Lady Michelle gestured Janet to walk with her.

It was hard to keep up with Lady Michelle's long legs but Janet managed.

"Me and my Husband might be members of the English Nobility but we have a side business too,"

Whatever it was Janet didn't want any part in it. From her years of experience, all side businesses were criminal and dodgy as any criminal gang. Hell, most the side businesses Janet had dealt with were ran by criminals.

She had to get the beads and escape.

"We are not criminals Janet,"

Damn! Janet had forgotten about the telepath thing. She had to remain focused and forget her thoughts.

"What is this side business?" Janet asked.

Lady Michelle looked around. "Coast is clear. You know the Anti-Supernatural Bill going through the Houses of Parliament and Lords at the moment,"

Janet couldn't believe she would even mention such an outrageous thing in a public place. The Bill, Act or whatever else the UK government decided to call it would ruin her and her business.

All Janet wanted was to make jewellery, sell it and give people joy in their lives. She wasn't going to hurt anyone, but just because a gang of five magic users decided to go round killing people, the UK

Government saw its chance to make magic illegal.

It was wrong!

Janet had wanted to move to Scotland more times than she cared to admit because their leaders seemed to like Magic Users. But it didn't matter in the end, if the UK Government made magic illegal then it would find a way to make Scotland make it illegal too.

The wonders of UK politics!

Janet frowned. "What about it?"

Lady Michelle looked around again. "Me and my husband are the only Magic Users in UK politics. The Bill will pass and our people will be doomed,"

Janet wanted to leave now. It would be Christmas in a few weeks, all she wanted to do was make her gifts and get on with her life. She didn't want to think about this.

"The Bill will be passed before Christmas," Lady Michelle said.

"Why tell me this? I am a simple Gift Maker,"

Lady Michelle smiled. "That is why I sought you out. Ever since I first met… brush your mind at university I knew you were different. You love the world, you love magic, you love your creations. I do not believe you want that to end on your watch,"

Janet hated when other people were right. Especially this Lady Michelle, Janet loved creating gifts, spreading the joy and showing others the wonders of magic. She didn't want to stop, she wasn't going to stop, no matter what the Law was.

Lady Michelle knelt in front of Janet. "I am

begging you Janet Oblong to help me,"

The sight of a Lady kneeling on the ground and getting dust and dirt all over her power suit was something, and Janet realised that these words weren't the act of a malice or manipulative woman.

These were the words of a scared woman who just wanted to do the best for her people.

"Rise Lady Michelle," Janet said, always wanting to say that. "What must I do?"

Lady Michelle got the beads out of her pocket.

"I need you to make a gift. I need you to make a gift that is so great for all 600 members of Parliament. Show the Elected Officials of the UK what magic can offer. Prove to them the power of magic and how joyous it is and show them how magic binds us all together,"

"What about the Lords?" Janet asked.

Lady Michelle smiled. "You deal with the Elected Officials. I will deal with the Lords personally,"

Janet took the beads from Lady Michelle, rushed back home and got to work on the gifts.

Time was running out for her kind.

***

Janet sat in front of her massive TV with her beautiful husband next to her as she watched all the Elected Officials of the UK Government vote on the Anti-Magic Bill.

Her small living room smelt of the lavender, scented oils and oranges that she had used to make all the gifts and now she hoped that her hard work had been enough.

She had made every one of them the best gift she could and Janet just hoped it was enough to make them support magic.

According to the News, this was the first time ever in Parliament's history that every single member had been present to take part in a vote. Normally that would have concerned her, but tonight she couldn't care less.

Janet gripped her husband's magically charged hands tighter as a tall man stood up on the television and read out the results.

Her heart was thumping in her chest as the next few seconds would determine her life, her husband's life and the life of her people.

"The Yeses have 2 Votes. The Noes have 598 Votes. The Noes have it. The Noes have it!"

Janet felt an immense wave of relaxation wash over her, but the sound from the television was deafening as every single (minus the two that voted yes) Elected Official jumped up and celebrated.

No one wanted magic to be outlawed.

And it was all because of Janet. Sure no one would ever know how she had saved magic, but Janet didn't care. She only cared about the making of her gifts, sharing the joy and most importantly showing people how magic binds everyone together in joy.

Whatever tomorrow was going to bring, Janet looked forward to it because she had saved magic, got the contract with Lord Michelle and now she was even helping Lady Michelle sell her gifts internationally as part of her side business.

But all that could wait.

Because tonight Janet was going to celebrate with the man she loved, and there was nothing that was going to stop her as she took him off to the bedroom for a long amazing night.

FANTASTICAL CHRISTMAS COMPLETE COLLECTION

INTRODUCTION
Mood/ Genre: Fantasy With Dark Theme

There are a lot of "rules" I have when it comes to holiday stories and these are the guidelines (that's what they are) that are shared by lots of writers. Holiday stories tend to be positive, fun and even when there are darker topics (like in the mystery stories in this Extravaganza). The topic isn't too dark.

But I have firmly decided to bend the rules slightly because this one is a tat dark, but it is a wonderful heart-warming story about something I am terrified of.

Being and dying in an old people's home. And dying of cancer.

I don't wish those things on anyone. Especially after a death in my family a few years ago.

But like all my stories this one has a wonderful happy ending that makes this difficult topic a joy to read.

So definitely turn over the page and start reading.

I can assure you, you don't want to miss this one!

ONE FINAL CHRISTMAS

The last thing I cared about was what the non-magic doctors were calling my cancer, they thought I had lung, bowel and bone cancer.

But they were wrong.

I couldn't blame them for being wrong, they weren't the specialist magic doctors like they had in certain parts of the world. These doctors in Southeast England were hardly that good at detecting magic.

I doubted they even believed in magic. That only made me feel more sorry for them, magic was an amazing thing to believe in, see and even touch it.

I hated the pain that shot through my bones every few seconds as the magical cancer pulsed through me towards my heart and brain. The cancer was going to kill me, I knew that for sure.

But as I turned on my soft cold hospice bed to look outside, I could only wish that I could pass through the window and go into that beautiful white snow.

The snow was falling quickly in massive flakes and on Christmas Day morning, the entire Southeast would wake up to a blanket of snow. It would definitely be a white Christmas.

That made me feel amazing.

I had always used my magic to make others happy. Poor children got rich, a dysfunctional family suddenly found a solution and the unfortunate became fortunate. All I had ever wanted to do was make others happy.

The smell of harsh chemicals mixed with the awful hints of urine made my stomach turn as my mouth filled with the taste of chemical lemons and I remembered how badly I wanted the cancer to take me. I was more than happy for the hospice to take me but I didn't realise everywhere would stink of urine, poo and chemicals.

A shot of pain pulsed up my spine and settled at the top, I didn't need to be told to know that the cancer was preparing to shoot into my brain and kill me.

The sound of the wind howling outside was like a siren call to me and I wanted, needed to go outside. But I was too weak from the cancer.

Why did I have to try and make a cursed family happy?

That's how you get magic cancer apparently. I was just walking along a long street at the time, saw a family frowning and decided I wanted to make their day. That was last Christmas. I cast a spell, it backfired horribly and pure dark energy shot into me.

That's when I realise the family had to be cursed by one of my magical brothers or sisters for something the family had done. If I had known then I would have left them, but I didn't. I tried to do the right thing and now I was dying.

I had even tried to reach out to my magical brothers and sisters and even magical parents, but they didn't listen to me. They probably thought I was trying to break magical law by trying to help out a cursed family. I couldn't blame them.

The sound of little paws tapping on the floor made me get up, bite down my agony and a wave of excitement filled me when I saw a ghost cat.

The cat was just as beautiful as I remembered with its long purple, blue and pink fur and its loud purring filling the room.

"My Familiar," I whispered as it stroked its cold ghostly fur.

My stomach relaxed as I stroked my Familiar again, it was great to see my oldest friend. The little cat had died years ago from old age, leaving me alone to bring joy to the world and Christmas cheer to all the good children.

I wished Familiar had been alive last Christmas, she would have known the family was cursed and stopped me. She would have saved me before I did what I always did, act first, think later.

Familiar brushed against my legs and I felt something. I felt as if she was urging me to follow her outside.

My heart skipped a few beats as I remembered something in magical law about the return of your Familiar and your death.

"It's time, isn't it?" I asked.

Familiar nodded and whipped her tail against the floor.

I looked outside in the snow. I so badly wanted to go outside, feel the snow a final time and walk over to the other side. But a tiny part of me didn't feel ready.

Then again, what did I have to live for?

I was stuck in some urine, poo and chemical scented hospice with no friends and no one to miss me. At least if I died outside, I would get to die on my own terms and once again be permanently reunited with my magical brothers and sisters.

"Come on then Familiar," I said, getting up.

I grabbed my awfully thin robe, old slippers and my ancient magical cap. At least the cap would allow me to die looking good, the only magic it had was the ability to make the wearer look stunning.

If I was going to die, I wasn't going to look like every other old fart in this place!

Familiar bounced outside my door and meowed for me to hurry up.

I went outside my room. I had always hated the cold sterile white of these long hallways, there was no love, respect or compassion here. The entire hospice was waiting for us to die so they could get rid of us and collect more money from the government.

Familiar meowed again. She bounced along the hallway towards the exit at the very end.

I shuffled along.

This was ridiculous. Last Christmas I would easily run down the hallway and be out of here within a minute, now I didn't know. I was so slow, I was so pointless, maybe my death would be a good thing.

I kept shuffling and Familiar bounced down towards me and bit me.

The pain didn't feel bad and Familiar injected me with some of her own blood, the pain felt nice.

Anything was better than the agony that kept pulsing up my spine as the magical cancer prepared for the final blow.

As mine and Familiar's blood mixed I felt a surge of power, energy and love fill me. I walked normally up the hallway but I heard Familiar bounce slowly behind me.

I didn't know how much blood she had given me but even ghosts could die in this mortal realm. I couldn't bear the idea of my oldest friend dying on me permanently.

My dream had always been to die and find her again in the afterlife. I dreamed of playing day and night with her like we used to.

But now she had decided I was the most important thing that she had to save.

The two massive wooden doors with two little glass mini-windows ahead of me led to the reception area and the exit. I went to push against them but I looked back at Familiar who was dragging herself over to me.

I dashed over to her, picked her up and pushed against the two massive doors.

They weren't moving.

They were locked.

I felt the magical cancer spiral up my spine slowly.

Familiar hit her head against my arm. She felt so cold, almost icy. But I felt the urge to throw her at the door.

I did.

She didn't even scream.

Then I saw her on the other side of the door and she meowed so loudly that I had to cover my ears. Thank the Magic non-magic humans couldn't hear her.

The two doors unlocked.

I hissed as the magical cancer bit into the base of my neck.

Familiar chomped on my leg.

Again I felt energy, strength and love fill me but I didn't like it. I didn't want Familiar to die. So I picked her up, walked through the reception area missing all the rows upon rows of horrible chairs and tables and pushed the exit door open.

A loud alarm started to go off and I kept walking.

The bitter freezing cold hung onto me as I went down the stone steps and into the snow covered road.

There weren't any cars about and the only sound was the defeating alarm so the sad truth was the hospice staff would be out here soon.

But I didn't care. I loved the amazing cold wind and snow that blow around me, chilling my skin and making my thin useless robe flap in the wind. Even the hints of Christmas spices in the air probably coming from a nearby house only made tonight even more magical.

Because now I could happily die knowing I had experienced one final Christmas with my Familiar out in the wonderful white snow and dying on my own terms.

Familiar gently tapped her head against my chest and I felt the urge to look back at the hospice. I instantly smiled when I saw my body dead on the stairs, surrounded by three hospice staff.

I kissed Familiar's head, savouring her beautiful purple, blue and pink fur because she had proved something to me. She might be weak because she wanted to save me so badly, but she was alive.

And now I was dead, I would take care of her like I always dreamed of, nurse her back to health and then we could play day and night like we both wanted.

Now this really was the perfect Final Christmas.

INTRODUCTION
Mood/ Genre: Dark(ish) fantasy

Whilst I am extremely happy to say that none of what happens in this story has happened to me, I want to mention that it does feature something that might put off readers if you're having a bad day.

However, this is such a great story from one of my favourite series, because if you study psychology (or are a psychologist) then you know there are so many myths, misconceptions and utter rubbish we have to deal with.

For example, people are obsessed with thinking we can analyse and know everything about them just by how they talk, and they think we are obsessed with their childhood.

Just no.

But then I decided, what if these myths were someone's superpowers?

So Matilda Plum quickly got born and this is one of her stories at Christmas time.

And if you enjoy this story then definitely check out her book *The Rogue God* coming out in mid-late 2023 on all major eBook and print booksellers. You definitely don't want to miss that great book!

Meanwhile download or turn over the page to read more about this wonderful story about being down on your luck, family and love.

As all good Holiday stories should be about!

Enjoy!

AUTHOR'S CHRISTMAS PROBLEMS

Even since I was born before The Great War I had always loved Christmas and how it had changed over the decades. I loved all the gift giving, the courting and the grand Christmas parties that use to happen last century, and I seriously enjoy the more modern Christmases too.

I always make sure I do my Christmas shopping early in December so it leaves Christmas Eve and Christmas Day free for me to go out and do my job.

And yes, it is a very fortunate factor that I get to work on Christmas day.

But thankfully Christmas Day was only three days away, and I was seriously looking forward to that.

My name is Matilda Plum, a superhero in the counselling, therapy and psychology sector. It is my job and utter passion to travel round helping people, solve their problems and maintain their mental health.

It's a great job and I love it.

I also love that Christmas time is both my busiest and quietest times of the year as everyone is filled with merriment, happiness and all that sense of goodwill crap that we teach children to believe in.

I was walking down a particularly wonderful stretch of Canterbury high street in England with the delightfully cold air blowing gently just chilling my skin enough to know it was cold, but not too much that I wanted to go home.

There were plenty of little shops with Christmas lights, decorative and free samples of mulled wine (I got so drunk going to all the shops sampling their goods one year). And the sound of people singing carols in the distance made me smile.

There was so much goodwill in the air that I loved it, but I was NOT letting carollers stop me, not when I had a job to do. Because in my opinion, carollers are the plague of Christmas, most of them can't sing, they're too bubbly and they won't go away unless you give them money.

I was just about to take my shopping bags, filled with fresh vegetables, meats and other things I needed for my annual Psychology Superheroes Dinner, into a very large kitchenware store (because my friends broke my roasting tins. Don't ask!) when I sensed something.

You see being a superhero psychologist meant all the myths and misconceptions about psychologists are my superpowers, and right now my spidey sense was telling me not to go in the kitchenware store but to go into the bookstore next door.

I looked at the large four-storey high bookstore for a moment with its tinsel, Christmas lights and Christmas displays in the window for a moment. And I did need to grab my friend Octavia, a superhero in the gambling sector, a book for Christmas.

So I might as well kill two birds with one stone.

As I entered the very large bookstore I was surprised at the sheer amount of little wooden tables in rows in front of me filled with brand new books from so many authors.

Then I noticed how the bookstore had ever so carefully created a pathway for readers to start looking at one genre and end up at the same table. My superhero powers were telling me there were so many little tricks here that made a customer behave like the owners wanted, that it was so clever.

Just not what I was here for.

But I did go over to the large table next to the counter to see what book the owners were trying to push so hard. I was rather underwhelmed, I had been expecting something sensational, maybe a romance, maybe a fantasy book but nope. It was only the latest book by a writer me and millions of customers had gone off.

I sneered at the book and heard the young woman behind the tills laugh quietly. I looked up and her and focused on her long brown hair, tasteful green uniform and long pink nails. She looked great.

"Am I not the only one to do that?" I asked.

The woman carefully moved her head in the direction of a security camera and I understood she didn't want to get into trouble and I understood that.

Since the woman had spoken to me, I used my analysis superpowers to learn that she was a very bright woman from a nearby university who just wanted to finish work on Christmas Eve and go home to her family up in London.

Yet she was concerned about whether or not she would have enough money for petrol.

As much as I don't believe that all humans do actually show the Christmas spirit, I know I always try. So I picked up the awful book on the table, went over to the young woman and subtly gave her a £50 note and bought the damn book too.

The woman subtly smiled and thanked me for the money and I was about to leave when she said something to me.

"You know the author's upstairs you know," she said.

My superpowers urged me to go up and talk to him.

I seriously didn't want to because the entire reason why me and millions of others didn't like his books anymore was because his stories were just so repetitive, the endings were rubbish and the author had turned to drugs.

Personally the whole drug thing doesn't bother me because I know he just needs professional people, but given how bad his books were getting. I didn't have time for bad stories, so I refused to read him now.

Yet I am a superhero first. I had to talk to him.

"Thank you," I said to the woman and I went upstairs taking my rather heavy shopping bags with me.

***

It took me another half an hour until I had finished searching the entire bookstore and found the author in a very dark corner of the bookstore surrounded by horror novels that were on clearance.

The author wasn't very tall, maybe five foot at the very most, he wore dirty blue (I think) jeans, a dirty t-shirt and shoes that must have been bought last century.

This really wasn't how I imagined this author looking.

Even though I was in what I call winter clothes wearing some black jeans, a long thick coat and with my hair dyed green (don't ask!). I still looked far, far better.

As I stood next to him, wanting to be sick at the smell of his cigarettes, weed and the musty books around us. I just wanted to help him, and help make his Christmas a little better.

"Hello?" I asked.

The man didn't even acknowledge who I was, I got out the book I had just bought because I needed to double check what his real name was. He wrote under the name Samuel Ratcliff, but it turned out his real name was Sam Jenkins.

"Sam Jenkins," I said.

Again Sam didn't even react to me.

I slowly started to hum a merry little Christmas tune to myself that was charged with superpowers and as it entered Sam's mind. I began to analyse and learn a lot about him.

Wow.

I knew from the newspapers and local news channels that he had had a rough time of late with drugs, some escorts and other things. But it turned out his wife had filed for divorce for cheating on her, he had spent his life saving on weed and his publisher was about to blacklist him from the industry.

And I knew it shouldn't have come as a surprise to me, but he was seriously starting to consider suicide.

Of course as a superhero I had to stop that, but I also had to somehow improve his life.

"Your wife isn't happy then," I said.

Sam slowly turned to face me. "How do you know? Did my publisher send you? I told them I don't want to write another fantasy mystery book,"

That was what I could use to help him.

"I am… a friend Sam, I was a reader actually,"

"Was?" Sam said.

I knew how upset he was knowing he had lost readers, but his emotion was so raw, painful and he wasn't happy in the slightest.

"I used to love your books. In the 90s they were

my bread and butter, I would run home from secondary school each day and my teenage self would read a new book,"

It was a complete lie considering how old I was, but it seemed to make him smile.

"I just can't go on. I hate writing. I hate my life. Even my own family hates me," Sam said.

And that was my path to helping him, I loved it when my clients (which Sam basically was at this point) basically told me how to help them.

Then Sam started to leave. "It was nice meeting you,"

A dark black aura formed around him, he was about to die.

I grabbed him. "You don't have to do this Sam. You can love your writing again, your fans love you still. Hell, I love you,"

Sam sighed, folded his arms and just looked at me. I knew I had some work to do.

"Please, whoever you are. Just... just let me go. The world will not even notice that I'm gone," Sam said.

I gestured to all the horror books on the shelves.

"People will miss you. Your family will miss you. Your kids will especially. If you do this then there is no coming back," I said calmly.

He really focused on all the books.

"I already," Sam said, "have a legacy. My books will be what people talk about,"

I had to laugh at that. Not very professional I

know, but I felt like it would prove a point.

And I seriously had to put down these shopping bags. I was laughing so much the bags kept shaking.

"What legacy is that Sam? People hate you and your books, but it doesn't have to be that way,"

Sam pushed away from me and he started to walk towards the stairs.

I focused my influencing superpowers to make him stop. He did.

"Then the world is better without me," Sam said.

I pretended to start crying. "But Sam! We need your stories. Your family loves you,"

Sam slowly started nodding. "I know you're lying about most of this. I don't know who you are but you can't help me,"

Wow! This guy was not making it easy for me.

I quickly searched his mind to see why his publisher kept making him write another fantasy mystery, and to my surprise they weren't. They were making him write whatever he wanted, it was Sam had didn't want to write.

Not the publisher.

"You really don't want to do writing anymore, do you?" I asked.

Sam nodded. "It's boring, lonely and awful. I want to be with my kids but the rewriting as much as I love it, takes so long,"

Well, I was really starting to feel like I couldn't save him, so I picked my heavy shopping bags up.

From what I understand about Sam Jenkins was

a man who lived for his writing, family and probably the so-called privilege that came from being a writer. He didn't want to write anymore, his family didn't like him and he clearly had no privilege left.

So I was going to have to make him do something for me. And it wasn't fun trying to hold some large shopping bags.

Making my superpowers as strong as I possibly could I sent into the deepest, darkest corners of his mind to and see his wife and take me with him.

Sam shook his head a few times then he hissed and looked at me.

"Actually, if you really think I can be saved. Come home with me, meet my wife and know how terrible of a situation I'm in?"

I pretended to act like I might be crossing a line.

"Please," Sam said.

Even I was surprised at the emotional pain in his voice. He really was at the end of his tether and I seriously didn't trust him to drive us home.

So I grabbed him and we teleported off.

I just needed to drop off my shopping bags first.

***

One of the best things about a superhero is when we teleport the world becomes blurry to people for a millisecond then it's like we were always there. People aren't surprised or don't even suspect we weren't there a second ago.

Sam thought the same thing.

He knocked on his front door, his wife frowned

as we entered and she led us into a very modern kitchen. It was rather lovely actually with its bright copper tones, kitchen island and red and green tinsel hanging from the lights.

Then the little tunes of Christmas playing softly in the background.

"What do you want? You stink of weed," the wife said.

As the two spoke (loudly) I tapped into my analysis superpowers and the wife only confirmed what I already knew. She really did love him, he was the centre of her entire universe and she hated doing this. But as she saw it she had to do what was in the best interest of their children and herself.

Then to edge things along, I implanted the suggestion of Sam getting on his knees and being truly vulnerable with his wife. Something he had never done before, and something she really wanted.

Sam did it immediately.

"Bertice, I love you more than anything else in the world," Sam said.

As Sam continued explaining himself, how he didn't want to be a writer anymore, how he felt so disappointed into himself and more. I had to admit Bertice was an awful name.

After a few moments Bertice knelt down on the ground to, they both kissed, said they would work things out and then she asked him how many roast potatoes he wanted on the big day.

After a quick cup of coffee, Sam showed me on

the way out and as me and him stood outside of their house, he asked me a question I didn't know how to answer.

"I don't know what you did, but thank you. I mean it. But who are you?"

"You're welcome," I said and gently kissed him on the cheek. "Happy Christmas,"

Then I teleported away and landed back in my very large, expensive bedroom and I just collapsed on my soft sheets.

I didn't know how to answer that question because I was so many things. A psychologist, a superhero, a saver and the rest. I did so much but I was always the person who was going to help the innocent, solve their problems and protect their mental health.

And whilst Sam might never write again, at least I saved him, and you never know he might write something, maybe something better than before and I really, really hope so.

But my friend Octavia was definitely getting that book I bought. I wasn't reading it, I wanted something new, exciting and different.

And I had a strange Christmas feeling that I wouldn't have to wait too long. Not long at all.

INTRODUCTION
Mood/ Genre: Contemporary Fantasy (With Dragons!)

If someone was to ask me what I think fantasy is, I really don't know how long it would take me to say dragons because I love them. To me, dragons are so amazing, mythical and they really do some up the fantasy genre.

I'm sure some of you have just rolled your eyes at me for daring to say that. But I really, really do love dragons so I wasn't surprised at all when I wanted to write this story.

And it is even a tat educational because it to refers some history that very few people know about, even the English themselves.

So of course, this is a very different take on the topic of dragons compared to what I normally write. For example, if you've ever read *The Winter Trilogy* or *The Aleshia O'Kin Fantasy Adventure Trilogy* (available in Early 2023) then you know I tend to write dragons as amazing characters with great personalities and fighting powers.

None of that happens in this story.

I won't say any more at risk of spoiling it but you will seriously enjoy this great story about immortality, revenge and love.

Enjoy!

LAST WINTER DRAGON EGG

Immortals die. You just need the right weapon.

Guardian Genesis Oakley stood at attention like she always did in her massive orange cave that rose so high into the sky that she was always interested in how much it was from the ground.

She never knew what happened above the ground too much these days. She knew who was in power, did they know about magic and the rest, but if someone asked her what the singers, celebrities or footballers of the world were. Then she would be useless.

Genesis utterly loved her cave with its massive feeling and appearance. She once timed herself actually running as fast as she could (which probably broke an Olympic record or two) and it still took her an hour to get from one side of her cave to another. So it would probably take a normal person four hours to run from one side to another.

Her cave was massive!

Genesis loved how the bright glowing crystals that grew out of the cave's domed ceiling illumined the cave with such natural intensity that Genesis never had to readjust her eyes when she went outside.

And combine that with the wonderful sound and refreshing taste of the natural spring water that flowed down the very, very end of the cave, it was simply the best place to live whilst she completed her duty.

Genesis always stood at attention in front of a very large pillar of solid granite with a single snowy white egg on top. It was easily twice the size of a normal human baby, and it contained one of the most precious things in the entire world.

A winter dragon.

Of all the dragons from the Chinese to fire-breathing to the Nature dragons and all the hundreds of different types in-between. Genesis had to admit her absolute favourite dragon was the winter one, well at least from the photos she had seen.

Genesis loved its snowy white scales, large pointy head like a snowplough and massive wings that were perfect for flapping away the snow. They were the perfect dragon for winter and that's why they were so loved and valued in Scotland, Iceland and Scandinavia.

Yet when the English invaded the Scots back in 1296, it didn't take them long to find the peacefully sleeping Winter dragons and a bunch of others that weren't a threat. But the English just killed them and then drank the dragon blood as a reward.

Genesis still laughed at that last part. Dragon blood was extremely poisonous to killers, if an innocent person drank it then it would cure them. But that was never going to happen to the English soldiers that slaughtered Scotland that year and every year since.

Genesis had been watching the Winter Dragons at the time, and laughing with her Scottish friends about the rumours of an English invasion. No one had wanted to believe the English would invade their neighbour just because they signed The Auld Alliance.

But they did.

As soon as Genesis saw the English coming, she grabbed a couple of dragon eggs (it was all she could carry) and ran as far as she could. She eventually found the wonderful cave she was in and now she was just waiting.

Waiting for the very last winter dragon to be born.

Genesis had watched the other egg she had carried away hatch hundreds of years ago but that dragon was ill, deformed and twisted.

It had died within ten years of life, but there was a reason why that still shocked Genesis to this very day. The dragon had transferred its life force to Genesis to make her immortal, so she could always watch over and protect the dragons.

Yet Genesis just knew that with the right weapon even immortals could and would die.

If anything else, her own immortality was a tiny piece of comfort compared to the only other gift that poor lovely dragon had given her.

For when she needed it most, Genesis would shoot fire out of her hands and form a flaming sword, and Genesis really hoped she had the power to summon other dragons but she wasn't sure.

She really wasn't sure on that part.

Genesis focused on the delightful warmth of the dragon egg in front of her as she watched it for a few more moments. She couldn't help but feel like something awful was about to happen, but she just had to focus on the egg in case she died.

Before the Winter Dragons were slaughtered, Genesis heard one of them mutter a prophecy that she really knew would come true throughout the centuries.

It was a rather simple prophecy for a dragon (Genesis realised centuries ago how complex some were!). It simply stated that one day, one winter, one moment near Christmas, an Englishman would come for the egg. If he won and took the egg, then dragons would become extinct within a hundred years and humanity would die too. If not, the dragons would never die and no humans would ever be hurt.

Genesis had always hated people who hunted and killed dragons. Thankfully so few people knew about dragons anymore, so very, very few people hunted them.

Yet Genesis had heard whispers of a group

getting more and more powerful and they were slowly (thankfully extremely slowly) revealing to the world the existence of dragons. And trying to convince them of them being dangerous.

Genesis just wanted to laugh at them. Dragons were no more dangerous than your domestic dog and cat.

The sound of cold heavy footsteps echoed throughout the entire cave and Genesis turned around.

Genesis kept a perfectly straight face as she focused on the terribly handsome man that stood ten metres from her. She just knew he had to possess some kind of supernatural speed to be able to travel that quickly from her secret staircase on the other side of the cave to where she was now.

The man was surprisingly handsome with his smooth middle-aged face, brown hair and tight fitting knights armour.

That little detail seriously surprised her, but considering she was wearing what could only be described as Jedi robes. She supposed she couldn't judge too harshly.

Genesis clocked the two large longswords in his hands and there was such a hungry in his eyes. This man just wanted to kill her and get the dragon egg.

The prophecy never went on to mention what the English did with the dragon egg if she failed. In fact, it only said that an Englishman would take it, it didn't say if the Englishman was working for the

English or someone else.

But Genesis had to stop him no matter what.

Genesis was about to say something to the man when she noticed something she couldn't quite understand. It was something in those cold dark eyes of his, she had seen them before.

Yes.

Genesis recognised those eyes from almost 800 years ago, she would recognise the sheer coldness of those eyes anywhere. Because this was the man who led the English troops to slaughter the dragons all those years ago.

This was the monster who robbed the world of so much beauty and this was the man who deserved to die for all the suffering he had bought her.

As much as Genesis didn't want to admit it, she had wanted to die naturally. She wanted to find love, have kids and live a life full of joy and wonder in Scotland, like all the other young women.

But no. Because this Englishman was such an idiot, fearful monster he had robbed her of all of it.

"You recognise me then traitor," he said coldly.

Genesis didn't even want to give him the respect of talking to him. Sure, she might have been English once, but when the war with the French had gotten to the point of being, well, pointless to some extent, Genesis had fled to Scotland in search of a new life.

That had quickly ended with the Auld Alliance. A rather innocent agreement to make sure that Scotland was always protected from the English, and France was too.

Genesis had met some of the Scottish clan chiefs and King John. They were great people. Sure, there were raids in Northern England but it did not mean an entire country deserved to be slaughtered because of one King's embarrassment.

"The egg will look nice over some toast," he said.

Genesis flicked out her wrists. Two flaming swords shot out.

"I will not allow you to do that. This is an innocent creature. Not that the English has ever cared about that," Genesis said.

The Englishman laughed. "What is such a *wee* woman like yourself gonna do?"

Genesis charged forward.

Jumping into the air.

The Englishman whipped out his swords.

He swung.

Genesis blocked them.

He kicked her.

Genesis stumbled.

The man shot forward.

Swinging his swords.

Genesis tried to block.

She failed.

The swords sliced her cheek.

Genesis flew at him.

Her swords flaming.

Sparks rained down on the cave.

The man hissed.

The sparks were engulfing him.

His skin burned.

Genesis kept swinging.

The man kept blocking.

The man jumped forward.

Knocking Genesis to the ground.

The man rammed his sword into her hands.

Genesis's flaming swords disappeared.

As Genesis screamed in crippling pain as she stared her hands with two swords rammed through them.

She couldn't move. She couldn't fight. She couldn't do anything.

Genesis wanted to do something but she was trapped. She was unable to do anything except hurt herself.

Genesis focused on shooting flames out of her hands. Yet she was in too much pain.

The Englishman laughed so loud that it harshly echoed around the entire cave and he went over to the dragon eggs.

Taking out a knife.

Genesis screamed in horror.

Blue flames shot out of her hands.

The swords glowed bright red.

Then white.

They melted.

Genesis laughed in delight as the swords melted around her but they didn't burn her. They formed themselves in two daggers for her.

Genesis grabbed them.

She charged.

The man spun around.

Whipping out a pistol.

He shot.

The bullet ripped through Genesis's stomach.

She slammed onto the cold ground.

Genesis tried to cope with the immense pain that filled her chest, stomach and soul as she felt her blood slowly gush out of her.

She hated this Englishman more than anything else in the world. All she wanted to do was protect this dragon egg so another life could be spared from this senseless violence.

That was never going to happen. Genesis knew that now.

She even felt her immortality and the remaining magic in her crackle away as Genesis realised that she wasn't shot with a normal bullet.

Genesis was going to die today.

"What do the Scottish bitches have on their toast?" the man asked. "Oh wait toast is probably too sophisticated for the barbarians,"

Almost 800 years had passed, the English no more respected Scotland now then they had all those years ago. Genesis hated that fact, she had travelled down to England two decades ago as she wanted to check in on the other dragon populations.

Yet she quickly returned to her cave and hurried back from London. The people there saw her as some kind of strange alien being that didn't deserve to be in *their* United Kingdom.

Genesis so badly wanted that to change one day.

Genesis felt the man stand over her. Pressing a blade against her throat.

"This is for all the Scots that my stupid country left alive that day," the man said.

Genesis wanted to point out there wasn't that many left. But it was a pointless comment. Then she heard something crack.

"How are you still alive?" Genesis asked, really playing up her Scottish accent.

More cracking echoed around the cave.

The man smiled. "If you torture enough dragons. One of them is bound to give you something,"

Genesis's eyes widened in horror.

The man raised the knife. He was going to end Genesis.

A white blur jumped on the man's back. It screamed. It roared. It chomped.

Blood splashed on Genesis's face.

The man screamed in agony as chunks were ripped from his back.

His head cracked.

Blood, muscle and brain matter painting the walls of the cave.

When the man's foul corpse slammed onto the cave floor, Genesis smiled when a very small, no bigger than a human child, snowy white dragon jumped onto her chest.

Genesis almost couldn't believe how beautiful it was, and because she had tried to buy the dragon as much time as possible. She had managed to keep it safe and buy it time to hatch.

The cute little dragon smelt so refreshing, piney and earthy as it raised one of its little claws and lovingly stroked Genesis's face.

But using the last remains of her strength, Genesis forced herself to lower the little dragon's paws. She knew exactly what it was doing, it was going to save her and sacrifice some of its life force to heal her.

She didn't want it.

For her mission was done. Her duty for the past 800 years had been to protect the dragons and make sure the last winter dragon egg hatched.

And now she had done it.

The little snowy white dragon kissed her and slowly nodded. Genesis was more than glad the amazing little dragon seemed to understand and immense coldness coated Genesis as the last of her life drained away from her.

Yet not before she saw the little dragon fly safely away so it could find a dragon pack and be loved and treasured and protected.

Genesis had done her job and now she could die happily and very, very proud.

INTRODUCTION
Mood/ Genre: Dark Contemporary Fantasy

I have always loved the Ancient Romans ever since school. I love their mythology, stories and how they managed to conquer a lot of territory. It is fascinating.

It's even more fascinating when ancient traditions from paganism get mixed with Christianity to create Christmas as we know it.

So since I first learnt about Saturnalia (the Pagan festival that Christmas is based on), I've always wanted to write a story on it, and now I have.

In this story, expect some modern pagans, fantasy and a massive problem. This is great fun and you're going to love this!

And if you don't know what Saturnalia is, don't worry. The story explains is perfectly.

Enjoy!

SACRIFICE FOR SATURNALIA

Kneeling on the cold soft mud surrounded by beautiful oak trees and bushes, I always have had a soft spot for English woodland. But I have to say that whilst I am far from a pagan, religious or anything to do with superstition. I love Saturnalia. I flat love it.

I love how the festival back in ancient roman turned society on its head by allowing a bit of chaos to spread. It's amazing how gambling, Masters serving slaves and other wonderous things were allowed on Saturnalia, but forbidden at all other times of the year.

That's why I love it. It was the one time of the night where the world could fall to chaos and everyone would celebrate it.

So when me and my witch and wizard friends mentioned recreating a Saturnalia for ourselves, who was I to say no?

Of course we weren't going to do the more religious side of the festival, but we were definitely going to take part in the gaff gift giving part. That was going to be amazing. I had already got all my friends a light up Santa who said rude things to them, that was perfect for my friends.

The cold howl of the wind chilled me as my knees sank further into the freezing mud as there was a small path in front of me in this woodland, where I was hoping that a small rabbit or something would cross so I could catch it for the Saturnalia.

The others might have said we didn't need a sacrifice to open the festival but I completely disagree. The sacrifice was the thing that kicked off the amazing feasts, gambling and the rest of the night. I had to have a sacrifice.

The smell of the cold air was filled with hints of damp, pine and sweet flowers as I peeked through the bushes to see if anything was coming along the path.

A lot of people might have believed (rightly) that this was a lot of trouble to go to for a silly outdated festival, but as much as I love Christmas with all the presents, food and family things. I suppose in a way Christmas is rather outdated considering we now know that Jesus was actually born in June and his birth was moved to combine with Saturnalia.

Leading to the creation of Christmas.

So this might be a lot of horrible effort for a festival, but I did want to impress someone special to me.

One of the young witches I know, Sandra, is stunning with her long golden hair, bright blue eyes and her wonderful body. She's amazing! Especially when it comes to her magic, she can do things I can't even imagine.

Anyway, she'll be there and I want to impress her. I want her to take notice of me. I want her to... maybe even talk to me.

It sounds silly but I really, really want her to like me.

A shriek echoed around the woodland.

I felt something sharp dig into the back of me.

I looked at the thing digging into me to see it was a knife and there was a tall woman pointing it at me. I tried to see what she was like but she was wearing an ugly large black cover and mask that covered all of her face except her bright blue eyes.

"What are you doing here?" the woman said firmly.

I recognised that voice. It was smooth, angelic and beautiful. I was glad it belonged to Sandra, but why the hell would she be here? She was meant to be cooking with the others.

"Sandra?" I asked.

The young beautiful witch took off her mask without even touching it, revealing her smooth stunning face that I wanted to kiss so badly.

"What are *you* doing here?" I asked.

Sandra frowned. "*I* wanted some herbs for a potion tonight. *You* aren't meant to be here,"

"I just wanted to get us a sacrifice tonight,"

Sandra rolled her eyes.

Great! Now she hated me. She wasn't going to

respect me, become friends with me and maybe in the far distance future fall in love with me. She was never going to be that!

A bird fell out of the sky.

Me and Sandra went out onto the path to have a closer look, but we both gasped. This wasn't a bird. It was a bleeding phoenix that was slowly turning to ash.

Sandra let her out her glowing blue magic and started to do something to it, but I could only stand there. The Phoenix was so beautiful with its shiny feathers. It didn't deserve to die.

"Damn it," Sandra said.

All the Phoenix turned to ash.

"It's okay. It will come back in a few minutes," I said.

Sandra shook her head. "Don't be silly. That's only if the ashes aren't scattered in those minutes,"

The wind started to blow.

Me and Sandra wrapped our arms around the ashes.

"Who could attack such a beautiful creature?" I asked.

"What makes you think it was a person?" Sandra asked.

"There was a perfect hole in the Phoenix. Nature isn't that perfect,"

I heard a rustle in the bushes and saw a shadow dash through the trees.

I was really starting to think that we weren't alone out here and I feared that we were going to be the sacrifice for someone else's Saturnalia, whether we liked it or not.

An arrow flew past my head.

Slamming into a tree.

Another flew past.

Catching my ear.

I jumped to one side.

Sandra hissed.

The wind flew.

Blowing the ashes away.

Sandra jumped up.

Someone whacked her over the head.

I looked up to see who had attacked her, only to see a fat horribly overweight man that smelt of sweat, urine and poo. I wasn't a fan of the massive crossbow in his hands. But what troubled me more was the humming like a choir of magical energy that radiated from the arrows.

"She'd make a fine sacrifice, don't ya think boy?"

For starters I'm 23 years old, and this foul bestial man was not having my Sandra!

I thrusted out my hand.

Only a few sparks shot out.

The man laughed. "Seriously? Are you even allowed to call yourself a wizard or warlock?"

I wasn't going to answer that.

"No matter boy. I'll take her, gut her and sacrifice her to the Glory of Saturn,"

Oh great of all the people to find out here tonight, I just had to find myself a hardcore pagan.

Normally pagans are wonderful people, I know tons of them, but this one seemed to be an extremist. Not fun!

"You won't take her!" I shouted.

The man clicked his fingers.

A sharp burning sensation shot up me.

"Saturn rewards me for my service. Me and my friends work each day to honour his Will. He ruled over the Earth once, he shall do it once more,"

Oh great. Not only was this man an extremist, he was a nutter too!

The man pointed the unloaded crossbow at me like he was trying to make a hard decision.

"Now the question is boy. Do I take you both as a better offering to Glorious Saturn?"

As much as I didn't want to answer, this felt like one of those times where whatever you say might be better than silence.

"I doubt it. Saturn will be getting a lot of sacrifices tonight. You can't overfeed him. Think of Saturn getting indigestion. If I was him I would be furious at the person who overfed me,"

The man clicked his fingers again.

I screamed.

"You! Dare to think what Glorious Saturn is thinking,"

He clicked his fingers again and again.

I screamed in agony.

"No," I muttered, as I saw one of Sandra's fingers twitch.

If I could just buy her a bit more time then I might be able to give her time to recover and attack. She was the more powerful one after all.

I held out my hand perfectly flat and willed a dancing flame to appear. It did. Only for a second or two.

The man laughed. "Ya pathetic boy. You couldn't even save a fly if your life depended on it,"

He was right. He was so right, I was worthless as far as magic was concerned. I had failed all my magic classes at school and if anything bad was to happen, I might as well have been a paper bag against a tsunami.

But I wasn't useless at everything.

"You know Mighty Chosen of Saturn, it might please Glorious Saturn if you teach me some magic,"

The man spat at me.

"Isn't the spirit of Saturnalia meant to be filling the world with a bit of chaos and turning the social order on its head?"

The man grunted and nodded. "Fine boy. The key to magic is just letting the Will flow through ya. Magic isn't ya enemy. It's a force. Don't resist,"

I willed the dancing flame to appear again. A bright blue, green and yellow flame danced against the wind for seconds before I stopped it.

I couldn't help but smile. "Wow, thank you!"

The man laughed and he had a strange look in his eyes. It was partly haunted, partly happy. As if he had taught other young people how to use magic before and loved teaching, then it was ripped away from him for some reason.

"Is your family celebrating Saturnalia with you?" I asked.

The man's smile disappeared. "No. My family... my family..."

I frowned and put my hands up in some sort of apology.

"I'm sorry. I didn't mean to bring it up,"

The man frowned. His eyes narrowed. He clicked four times.

Crippling pain filled me.

I fell on my back.

I clutched my stomach.

The man rushed over.

He stomped on my stomach.

Again and again.

Sandra shot up.

Thrusting out her hand.

Magic energy shot out.

Slamming into the man.

It exploded against him.

The air hummed with magical energy.

The man whipped out his crossbow.

He fired.

I jumped up.

Shooting out my hand.

I willed the arrows to stop.

They melted.

Sandra thrusted out her other hand.

Even more energy slammed into the man.

He screamed.

The energy turned to fire.

The man screamed as his body charred, smouldered and turned to ash.

When Sandra lowered her hands, she looked at me and smiled. In the years I had known her, she had never ever looked at me. And right now, she was. She was giving me a massive smile.

"You did well I guess," she said, something in her voice making it sound playful.

The pile of ashes were blown away in the wind and I couldn't help but feel sad for the man in a way. He must have lost his family, fallen into depression and found an Extremist Pagan group as support. It was a shame he didn't have someone to support him, something I never wanted my friends to have.

And that was the true reason I loved Saturnalia. Yes there was all the social order turning and the chaos of it, but it was really just an excuse for a celebration to spend time with friends, family and those you would never celebrate with normally (like the Masters and the Slaves of ancient Rome).

But this man and his friends had forgotten that. They shouldn't have wanted to kill anyone tonight, they should have wanted to celebrate with them and enjoy their company.

As I stared at stunning Sandra who still looked even more beautiful despite being whacked over the head with a crossbow, I realised that that was exactly what I wanted to do.

I didn't care about getting a sacrifice for Saturnalia, I just wanted, needed to go and see my friends and celebrate with them. And in a way I suppose I did have a sacrifice for Saturnalia after all, maybe Saturn would enjoy feasting on the man's soul or whatever he feasted on.

So at least the man did get his wish to meet Glorious Saturn wherever he may be.

Sandra started to walk away along the woodland back to the town and back to our friends, but she stopped and held out her hand to me. I didn't know if she was going to shoot fire or magical energy at me.

Yet I took it and she held my hand tight.

I didn't know nor care why, I just enjoyed it and looked forward to where tonight was going to lead us, but I hoped whatever Sandra's interest in me was, it was going to last for a long, long time.

FANTASTICAL CHRISTMAS COMPLETE COLLECTION

INTRODUCTION

Mood/ Genre: Light Contemporary Fantasy

For the next story in the holiday Extravaganza, I really wanted to explore a very fundamental question about the holiday season, love and death.

If you could talk to a loved one again, would you do it?

Now I fully appreciate that this might not sound like a very light topic for the holiday season, but given how the holidays are meant to be about love, family and friends. I don't really think there is a better topic for this time of year.

So in this next Extravaganza story, please expect a grieving man, some souls and most importantly some magic.

Enjoy!

SOULCASTER

Snow crunched under my feet as I walked through the beautiful snowy forest, I loved the way the snow blanketed the massive tall pine trees like it was some winter wonderland. This was the first time in years I had felt... good, maybe even good since my wife died, and yet I was here to do something silly.

Up ahead I saw a bright flickering fire with tall shadows of people walking around it, I looked forward to the amazing warmth of those tall flames, anything was better than the bitter cold that was trying to bite at me.

Now I was never a religious person, I hated religion with a passion, but I supposed I had grown so sad, miserable and depressed over the years since my dear sweet wife died, I had grown too desperate.

The smell of cold smoke filled the air wonderfully as it reminded me of my delicious favourite barbecues as a child. I got close to the roaring fire and I started to hear little whispers from the people round the fire.

I knew I had probably gone crazy when I had checked out the online advert for the so-called Soulcaster that could apparently make my life better and allow me to speak to my dead wife one final time.

Absolutely rubbish.

But I saw the online advert a few more times and I guess I got worn down so I clicked on it, checked out the details and decided to come here.

All I knew for sure was this Soulcaster woman (or man) was meant to be some kind of ancient person who had direct ties to the Pagans. Well, given it's the freezing dead of winter in the southeast of England, I suppose it had to be pagans or whatever.

Not that I know anything about the pagans.

I got closer to the fire and I couldn't understand it but it looked as if the entire fire had changed since I last focused on it.

Now the fire looked larger with tens of tall, short and medium sized people around it holding out their hands to get warm. I couldn't blame them. It was freezing out here, apparently the canopy in the forest was meant to give it some warmth but that clearly wasn't happening.

I heard the whispers clearer now and even then I didn't understand. Normally I could understand everyone, no matter how bad their English, but these whispers, these people weren't speaking English. It sounded Latin or something.

Something in the back of my mind wanted me to

turn around and never ever return here, but there was a part of me that wanted to continue. It was probably the part of me that decades working as a scientist had developed and matured.

I had to know what was going on here.

I walked straight up to the fire and looked at its roaring, swirling and whirling flames that dramatically rose and fall in defiance of the natural wind that was blowing. But what made me even more curious was how the person in all their different sizes, heights and ethnicities weren't looking or taking any notice of me.

That was strange.

I looked around and wondered what they were doing, there was no one else around me but still all these people were staring at the fire and whispering in Latin to each other.

Now something inside me was telling me to leave but then I started to hear something like a whooshing sound behind me.

I looked around and saw a massive Christmas tree appear with thousands of lights, baubles and golden tinsel hanging off the tree perfectly. I couldn't believe my eyes, the tree was so beautiful, perfect and filled the air with the joyous hum of Christmas Spirit.

Walking over to it, my eyes narrowed and I was determined to figure out what this was. I had to channel my inner scientist because there had to be a logical explanation to this, the tree wasn't there a moment ago, and out of all the strange things I had seen in my life this had to top the list.

"Do you know what Soul Day is?" an old lady said to me.

I blinked and jumped.

A little old Lady was hunched over in front of me wearing an ugly long dark cloak with massive holes. I wanted to offer her my own coat or offer her something to help her, I didn't want to see an old lady cold on this night.

But the more I looked at this old lady, the older she appeared to be.

She raised her head slightly and my eyes widened when I saw how dead, glassy and lifeless her own eyes were. It was almost like her eyes were dead and yet she endured.

Now I mention it, her face looked pretty dead too. Her skin was dry, broken and cracked.

As much as I wanted to offer my help (I always want to help people), I got the sense from her that it was safer not to get too close to her.

Then I remembered the question.

"Soul Day?" I asked.

"Yes young man," she said.

I wanted to laugh at that, I wasn't young, I was ancient according to my grandchildren and all the neighbour kids.

"Soul Day is the day better than Christmas," she said.

I doubted it, for me Christmas was the only day I felt alive, happy and like life was worth living. I got to see my children, my grandchildren and spend quality time with them. To me that was the most precious thing ever.

"Soul Day is when all the souls of the dead come to us once more and we can listen," she said smiling at me.

I wanted to ask her so many questions, about my wife, my family, my future, but I didn't push her. Whoever she was I got the feeling it was better not to push her, and instead just let her do the talking.

"You come here because someone wills it. I can see something in you. A shadow. A Loom. No, sorry, a looming death. A wave of sadness that claims your family and destroys all their Christmases to come,"

My mouth dropped. I didn't want that for my family, I wanted them to enjoy life, be happy and merry. They didn't deserve to be sad.

The woman extended a long pointy finger and pointed at my head.

"You're going to die,"

That was impossible for this random stranger to know, I hadn't told anyone presides my own family and they wouldn't tell anyone. I had only found out about the brain tumour a few weeks ago and the doctors said it might still be treatable so they needed to do some more tests.

"Whoever wills you to come here is here. They walk through the forest. The cold snow biting at their feet. They come here to speak to you,"

I wasn't having any of this nonsense coming from the woman. It was impossible for her to know anything, she couldn't have known about my tumour, she couldn't have known anyone was coming and she couldn't have known anything about me.

I didn't even know her.

"Leave me alone," I said walking towards the fire.

But I stopped as soon as I saw the fire had changed yet again with the flames still roaring but the flames were smaller, blue and colder.

"What is this place?" I asked.

I felt the old lady's body warmth against my back but I didn't feel her press into me.

"Look at the people," she said.

As I looked at them I didn't see anything special about them. There were so many people in all their different sizes, heights and clothing that there wasn't anything too interesting to see. Except one thing.

They weren't speaking Latin anymore.

Instead they were just standing there staring straight at me like I was the only thing in the world at that point.

"Why are they staring at me?" I asked.

"They see something in you. They see the same as me. We all see a looming death,"

"What is all this? What is Soul Day?" I said firmly.

The old lady laughed. "Soul Day is what you make it. It is meant to protect your Soul. It is meant to kill it. It is meant to save it,"

I threw up my arms in disbelief. Whatever this

weird online advert was meant to be, it was clearly meant to be some sort of prank, lie or whatever.

I didn't care anymore.

I was going home.

"Hubby?" a young woman said behind me.

As I looked at the woman my eyes widened as I stare the ghostly form of my late wife, her skin youthful, her hair long and golden and her clothes exactly like the night I met her in the 60s.

Her face looked so beautiful, calm and stunning but I didn't want to believe this was my wife. My wife, my stunning wife was dead, this couldn't be her. There was always a logical explanation and her being alive was not one of them!

"You see the shadow. The Loom. The Looming Death over him," the old lady said to my wife.

My wife frowned. "I do. Hubby, what is wrong?"

I saw the old lady walk away. "You aren't real. My wife is dead. I don't care what your acting school is paying you, don't pretend to be the dead!"

"You always were a scientific one. You never did believe in anything else. I am here hubby,"

As much as I wanted to believe it was her, I couldn't. There were no such things as ghosts, monsters or the supernatural. My wife couldn't be in front of me unless she was a pile of ash.

"I'm leaving. Good luck with your acting classes. You're good, I'll give you that,"

I was about to walk far, far away from this strange, god forsaken place when the old lady appeared holding out a large golden Bauble.

I'll admit it was beautiful with the stunning reflection of the dancing flames but again that wasn't possible. The flames were so small.

Then I looked at the fire.

All the people were gone and the fire was a raging inferno. The sound of the flames was deafening and now I sank to my knees in confusion.

"Please. What is happening here?" I asked my voice full of emotion.

My wife knelt next to me. "I wanted you here tonight. In the Place-After-Earth, I got to see what became of my family,"

I looked at her, my eyes watery.

"Hubby. You die soon. Our family falls apart. Some hate you for being so grumpy, sad and depressed. Some defend you. All fall to pieces. All turn to ash. Our Family ends,"

That wasn't true. I was a great person and everyone understood that my wife had died and I was finding life hard. They wouldn't hate me. They...

My wife held my hand. I almost jumped at the coldness.

"Hubby. When you come here and are reunited with me. What do you want to watch from above? Your family fall apart or your family love each other, celebrate and respect you,"

I didn't know what to say. I still couldn't believe this was my wife, my stunning wife that I had loved for decades and mourned for so long recently.

But there was something in her voice that made it all sound so truthful.

My wife disappeared to be replaced with a large ball of golden swirling light. The light rushed past me. I saw it go into the golden bauble the old lady was holding.

"Bring her back!" I shouted.

The Old Lady laughed and gestured me to stand up.

"You still want to know what Soul Day is truly about?"

I nodded.

"The Shadow grows within your head. The Looming Death grows ever closer. The Tsunami of Sadness grows stronger every second ready to consume all those you loved,"

"Please. What must I do?" I asked.

"Soul Day is the one time of the year where I come out from the past and into the future. The veils between the past, present, future and the living and the dead are so weak. Not even paper thin. So I picked this year to come and I willed thirteen people to come. And you are the last,"

I felt my stomach tighten.

"What happened to the other twelve?"

The Old Lady shook her head. "They forsaken me. They choose to spend Soul Day by spending their souls and damning their world to grief, terror and misery,"

"I won't," I said more out of instinct than

thought but I still smiled.

The Old Lady nodded. "Then change. You have exactly three months to live. I will come knocking in the dead of the night. So you love, respect and adore your family or your soul will be damned,"

I couldn't do anything but nod and smile to that. It sounded crazy, stupid and silly but it also sounded so right, like it was the truth and nothing else was going to convince me otherwise.

I knew I had to go home call my family, invite them round for dinner tomorrow and make sure tomorrow was the start of a wonderful final three months.

"Thank you," I said to her. "I'll make sure my family hear the story of Soul Day and why it is the most important Day of the year,"

The Old Lady smiled and slowly started to disappear.

"Then go but never forget the Shadow. The Looming Death. Nor the Tidal Wave of Sadness. It will come but only you can stop it. So love, respect, adore your family til we meet again,"

As I left the strange fire, forest and the Soulcaster, I was going to be the greatest father, grandfather and person in the world to make sure my family were going to be strong after I died.

But about the whole Soul Day thing, I actually think it could be the start of something great and an amazing legacy for me and my family. Because at the end of the day, my family are my love, my life and my future.

AUTHOR OF THE FIREHEART FANTASY SERIES

CONNOR WHITELEY

SOLSTICE GUARDIAN

A HOLIDAY CONTEMPORARY FANTASY SHORT STORY

INTRODUCTION
Mood/ Genre: Light(ish) Contemporary Fantasy

As we're near the two-thirds mark of the Holiday Extravaganza and we've had the vast majority of the fantasy short stories, I think. I feel like I should mention a little funny fact, I used to believe I would never ever write contemporary fantasy.

I don't really know why, but it was probably because I didn't like to read it, and I (stupidly) didn't really believe contemporary fantasy was "real" fantasy.

Of course I don't believe it now, but I did.

However, I'm really glad I've gotten over that silliness because I do really enjoy writing all types of fantasy and different genres.

Moving on to today's story. There is literally no other topic I could have written about because to me as a fantasy writer, the winter solstice is so iconic, mythical and magical.

There are so many stories I could write about this

special event, but I decided to write one in one of the most iconic locations.

Stonehenge.

If you love the Winter Solstice, pagan inspired stories and magic. You seriously don't want to miss today's story.

Read it now!

SOLISTICE GUARDIAN

Alecia flat out hated the Winter Solstice.

It was such a stupid holiday that silly people celebrated and only believed it was made up. But it wasn't, and it was that that annoyed Alecia more than she ever wanted to admit.

To most people the Winter Solstice was just another day and some people believed it was magical, but they clearly had no idea what it actually involved.

To Alecia, it was the one stupid day of the year she got to return to life, but all the Gods and Goddesses only allowed her to do one pointless thing. Defend humanity against the demons, ghosts and other supernatural forces that tried to attack humanity through the Thinning of the Veil that always happened during this pathetic holiday.

Alecia hated it.

She would have been perfectly happy to return to life, maybe she would like to defend humanity, but every single year? It was just getting old.

And it didn't help that Alecia hated the massive stone blocks of Stonehenge and how they were placed on top of each other to create doorways for the supernatural forces to walk through.

That is what she hated.

She hated how pointless the Winter Solstice truly was. No matter what she did, the supernatural would only come round next year and try again to attack. Alecia kept fighting, suffering and hurting only for the damn supernatural to return like it was nothing.

Even the air was annoying with its sweet piney scent that reminded Alecia of amazing smoky dinners round the campfire as a child (which she barely remembered at this point).

So this year Alecia decided to sod all the Gods, Goddesses and the Supernatural, all they had done was screw her over year after year, decade after decade, century after century. Maybe even longer, Alecia didn't remember.

Alecia loved the coldness of the English countryside around Stonehenge with its pitch darkness, large open fields and even a disgusting "Motorway" (whatever that was) right next to it.

Even that "car" sound with so many of the futile metal boxes with wheels flying past didn't sound right. The sooner Alecia was done the better!

As much as she loved how the cold made her feel alive after a year of death, her soul floating through all of time and space waiting to either be devoured by the supernatural or resurrected by the so-called (foul)

Divine Ones. Alecia just wanted to sod all the Gods.

She was going to destroy Stonehenge.

That way none of those stupid supernatural forces could attack and that foul, disgusting Gods and Goddesses could no longer resurrect her.

Alecia could finally die.

She loved the idea of that. Finally just a chance to enjoy her death, feel nothing and eventually have her soul diffuse out so she was truly dead.

Alecia walked over to a large stone that looked like an altar in the middle of Stonehenge and ran her fingers over it. The icy coldness that shot into her felt wonderful. Normal people might have moaned at the pain it caused them, but to Alecia it was amazing, like little needle pricks on her numb body.

From what she had learnt (or rather her soul had learnt) whilst she drifted, Stonehenge was the only gateway left on Earth where the Veil thinned enough for the supernatural to walk through.

It had to go.

But Alecia had only heard fragmented whispers of stories about how other people had destroyed the other gates.

Perhaps the Gods and Goddesses knew more about the gates and how they were destroyed, but Alecia really didn't want to talk to them unless it was absolutely necessary.

And considering that Alecia was trying to find a way to circumvent their will so she no longer had to fight with her trusty sword, she was never going to ask them.

With the icy coldness starting to weaken in her fingers, Alecia remembered how the other people had destroyed the gates. Apparently she had to make it destroy itself and convince the so-called spirit within to kill itself, so the gate could no longer exist.

It was completely stupid, the entire idea of spirits, ghosts and the supernatural was pure fantasy, but if Alecia had learnt anything over the past Gods-know how many times she had been resurrected, it was how fantasy was normally Truth. Regardless of what other narrow minded humans believed.

Alecia traced the shape of a pentagram on the freezing stone as she remembered what the fragmented souls had told her to say.

"I Alecia, Solstice Guardian, orders the Spirit of the Stonehenge to Come Forth and Reveal Themselves to Me,"

Nothing happened.

Now this was just silly, Alecia didn't want to be here, saying pointless made up words that made her look stupid if there were other people here. If she could, she would happily make a bomb, strap it to the stone and blow the whole damn place up.

But that wouldn't work sadly and Alecia hated the Gods even more for it.

A whoosh echoed around her.

Alecia was hoping it was nothing but she looked at one of the Stone Doorways and it was swirling, twirling and whirling bright pink energy.

Whoever had told her about that saying, Alecia swore she was going to kill that person again herself. Whoever it was had clearly lied, those words didn't summon the Spirit. It summoned those damn ghosts, demons and other supernatural idiots.

A deafening roar ripped through the English Countryside and Alecia whipped out her sword.

If this was the supernatural she was going to gut them, cut them and chop her way through them.

If Alecia failed, then she was going to send a clear message to whatever was in charge of the supernatural that she was not to be messed with.

A Reptilian Man with massive scales walked out of the Stone and stared at her.

Alecia pointed her sword at him. "Go Back. I do not want to fight you. Just go back,"

The Man licked the air. "Not what I remember. You summoned me. We should be quick. Others will be here soon,"

Alecia couldn't believe what she was seeing. The other Souls had always described Spirits to be human, ghostly or made of flesh and blood. Not scaly in the slightest.

"Aren't you ever tired Spirit?" Alecia asked.

The Man licked the air again and again. "I know what you seek. What you want. But I never fatigue. I never sleep. I never rest. The Last Gate Endures,"

Of course this stupid place has a dramatic name. Alecia couldn't believe it, of all the names this place could have it had to be some overdramatic one that meant it was going to be impossible for her to overcome.

"What do you mean the Last Gate Endures?"

The Man looked like he was eating the air. "The Last Gate. This place. The way for the Dead and Supernatural to come to us. It must endure. You depend on it,"

Alecia rolled her eyes. "I don't want to live. I want to die. I want to actually die!"

"You don't mean that. I have watched your soul float about. Talking to Others. Listening. Learning,"

Alecia couldn't believe this guy. How dare he think he actually knew her.

"Believe me Spirit. I want to die. I don't want this life. Being alive for only one day. And a terrible day at that,"

"You see other Souls as I do. You are not fragmented. The Supernatural hate you. They want you to die,"

Alecia threw her arms up in the air. "I am not being influenced by the Supernatural and so what if they hate me. I hate them. I hate the Goddesses and Gods. I hate you!"

The Man gestured to the English Countryside.

Alecia still loved that icy coldness that chilled her skin and made her feel alive, even if it was only for a few more hours, Alecia loved the almost painful coldness of the English countryside.

"What!" Alecia shouted.

"You might hate all this. They need you,"

"Who?" Alecia said, a lot of softer than she wanted to.

"The humans. Your kind. Those Narrowed Minded Fools,"

Alecia didn't want to entertain that idea. Even if the humans wanted or needed her, for one, they wouldn't believe she existed and two, she didn't want them.

The entire reason why she was dead in the first place was because of the selfish humans that let her die, they could have saved her.

But her death was acceptable. Even if her husband, lover or whatever the man she remembered was left grieving for her loss.

"I do not want them," Alecia said, her voice cold.

The Man grabbed the air and chomped on it.

"You think that matters? You actually do. Do you want to know me? You don't,"

Alecia shook her head at this Spirit. He was just strange. There was no other word for it.

"There once was a man called… I forget now. He had a wife, a Lordship and a belief. He did not want to lead, but he did not want to die. The Gods gave him a choice to serve or die,"

Alecia had no idea why this silly brat was talking about himself like this. She still hadn't bought down her sword.

"So once was a man who choose to serve. He became a spirit. And was stuck here,"

Alecia walked over to him ignoring the swirling,

whirling, twirling mass of pink energy behind him.

"What is your point?"

The Man licked his scaly lips. "My point is we all have purposes we do not want,"

Alecia smiled. "Then die. Destroy the gate! Be free!"

The Man shook his head. "There was a woman called Alecia, she did not listen. So she failed. She did not win. So she died. But she returned next year,"

Alecia pointed her sword at his throat. "Speak plainly or I will happily kill you,"

The Man clicked his fingers.

Her sword flew out of her hands.

Flying into the pink energy.

"Will you?" the Man asked.

Alecia walked over to the stone altar and allowed the wonderful icy coldness to claim her as she laid down.

"What is the point of all this? I am the Solstice Guardian but what am I protecting?"

"And that is the true topic of tonight. You want to know why you do this. Why it is you. Why you return but you watch others truly die,"

Alecia turned to look at him. "Why?"

"Strange the world is. I died on a Winter Solstice. I was not chosen as a Guardian. Instead I died here at Stonehenge. I died on the stone you lay on,"

That was just disturbing. Why the hell tell her something like that! But Alecia didn't want to move, she was savouring the pain of the icy coldness for the next year.

"I'm sorry for your death," Alecia said.

"I yours. But I died so my Soul could thicken the Veil between the worlds. You defend the Veil. We need each other. I need you for your defence, you need me to return you,"

"What!" Alecia shouted.

"The Gods and Goddesses do the resurrections. I still choose you every year,"

Alecia slammed her fists against the stone. "You're why I can't die! You little-"

"I like seeing you every year. It reminds me what beauty looks like. It reminds me of what I lost Alecia,"

That voice. The smoothness of those amazing words, she remembered them, she felt them, she knew what they were.

It was completely strange, stupid and chaotic but that voice was so familiar to Alecia.

She remembered.

"Alexon?" Alecia asked.

The Reptilian Man smiled. Then his scales fell away one by one, a few at first, then all at once. Revealing a tall beautiful man with perfect cheek bones, amazing hair and the most stunning of smiles.

This couldn't have been her husband, her lover or whatever he was (the resurrections had dulled that part of her mind), but it was all true and Alecia loved it.

She got up and touch Alexon. His skin felt icy

cold like the air, but it was real. Her fingers caressed each part of him and for the first time in all her afterlife, she felt alive and she actually felt something.

The sound of metal clagged against the stone altar.

Alecia loved the sight of the two metal swords.

"So my love, ready to Guard the Gate for another year?" Alexon asked.

She wanted to say to him how little, pointless and pathetic the entire Winter Solstice was, but she couldn't get the words out.

Alecia wanted to keep feeling, being alive and enjoying her death, and that only felt possible with Alexon at her side, so even if what she feared did come true and she fought tonight and died for another year.

Alecia didn't mind.

She would return next year, feel alive with Alexon and die again. It was the cycle of life and now she had Alexon, life was worth living.

Even if it was only for a single night.

FANTASTICAL CHRISTMAS COMPLETE COLLECTION

AUTHOR OF THE FIREHEART FANTASY SERIES

CONNOR WHITELEY

WEIRD FIRST CHRISTMAS

A HOLIDAY FANTASY SHORT STORY

INTRODUCTION
Mood/ Genre: Contemporary Fantasy

I'm sure lots of people can remember the time when their and their partner spent their first Christmas together in your own place. Maybe it was a flat, a house or a cottage.

And you were all caught up in making your own little Christmas traditions, decorating your tree and really looking forward to spending the holiday season together (and maybe a lot longer together).

Well that's far too normal for the Extravaganza!

So let's change this perfectness up a little bit. Let's throw in some magic, biscuits and a dragon and let's see what happens.

Shall we?

You really don't want to miss this next great story.

Enjoy!

WERID FIRST CHRISTMAS

Michael loved the warm, bright colours of the Christmas decorations as he hung them on the 6-foot tall Christmas tree with its large branches covered in fake snow. It was clear the snow was fake but it was beautiful in its own special way.

As he heard *Deck The Halls* playing quietly in the background and the smell of sweet gingery biscuits filled the air, Michael couldn't deny this was going to be a magical Christmas.

Michael finished hanging a blue bauble on the Christmas tree and went to search the cardboard box for another decoration when he saw there were none left. He looked around the large living room of his flat with its black walls and bright white three piece suite, but there were no more boxes.

Michael tried to remember what decorations he was missing, there had to be more than this, normally when he did the tree by himself, it took him at least an hour to get out all the decorations, find the perfect place for them and do the lights.

He had only been doing it for half an hour this year.

The hour might have seen like a long time to lots of people but Michael wouldn't have it any other way. He loved it. It was all part of the wonderful Christmas magic of the season, with the singing, decorating and spending it with his family.

Michael frowned at that idea. His family had abandoned him a long time ago because of his taste in men, and now every year he had to decorate his flat by himself with no one to help, support or love him in the holiday season.

It was one reason why he used to hate the holidays, as so many people banged on about how the season was all about love, eating and family. But when that family stops loving, kicks you out of their house and makes you have to beg for food, he quickly stopped loving the Holidays.

The sound of someone banging and tapping and baking in the small flat kitchen reminded Michael that this Christmas might be as magical, special and loving as the Christmases from his Childhood.

Michael went out to the kitchen and instantly loved the amazing ginger hints that filled the air, it was wonderful how such a little spice could make the entire flat smell intoxicatingly of the Christmas spirit.

Michael stared at the equally amazing man in the kitchen who was bent over getting something out of the oven, it was a great sight and it reminded Michael even more of how lucky he had been this past year to find Thompson.

Granted he hated the tale of how they met and knew how lame it was compared to other people's stories, but they met on a freezing cold night in late January early in the night, they spoke when Michael was on the streets and soon they developed something.

Michael still wasn't sure what to call it, a friendship, a romantic friendship or the most wonderful combination of the two. But whatever it was, he was more than happy where it had led him.

The sound of Thompson putting even more gingery biscuits on a wire cooling track made Michael walk over, hug Thompson and stare at the amazing biscuits.

If he had known Thompson was baking biscuits in the shape of dogs, cats and people, he would have bought more icing of different colours.

But something felt off about them.

He couldn't place it but Michael felt as if there was something different about the biscuits. It wasn't their colour that was for sure, these biscuits were your everyday brown (slightly) burnt colour that everyone knows and loves.

Michael couldn't shake the feeling that something was wrong.

Then a biscuit moved.

Michael grabbed Thompson's hand.

"Babe what is you put in those biscuits?" Michael

asked.

Then all the little biscuit dogs stood up, barked and jumped off the kitchen worktop.

"Babe?" Michael asked.

Thompson stared at the biscuit dogs. "I donno. Got this ginger powder from a woman at the market. She'd said it'd make our night interesting. I thought she meant sex,"

Michael playfully hit him around the head. This was not what he wanted tonight, he wanted to finish up the tree, snuggle up with Thompson on the sofa and enjoy his first Christmas ever with another man.

That clearly wasn't happening.

A pack of biscuit dogs ran up to Michael. Licking his ankles.

"It seems they like ya," Thompson said.

Michael didn't know what to do. This wasn't natural, was he hallucinating? Had he been drugged?

Then all the biscuit cats jumped up, meowed and jumped off the worktop only to start being chased by all the dogs.

The sound of the cats and dogs was deafening, Michael knew it was impossible for all the biscuits to be making the same sound. This was beyond normal.

"Are you baking anything else?" Michael asked.

Thompson held his hand tighter.

"What are you baking now?"

The oven jerked.

"What!" Michael shouted.

They looked at the oven to see something inside

banging against the glass.

"I thought it be fun to cook a dragon biscuit. Ya know your favourite animal and all,"

Michael pulled Thompson away from the oven. Whatever was happening this was no longer cool, entertaining or anything, this was just plain scary. He wanted to find a solution to stop these crazy animals but he was out of ideas.

He kept focusing on the possible dragon that was inside the oven trying to break free.

Normally Michael loved dragons, they were cool, epic and exciting. Dragons were in all of Michael's favourite films and all the heroes had to defeat dragons so this was part cool, part not. But today they were just scary!

The oven cracked open.

Then Michael watched five biscuit claws reach out of the crack and rip it open, making it bigger.

"Babe," Michael said.

A few seconds later a biscuit dragon the size of two footballs had crawled out of the oven. Michael had to admit it was stunning, Thompson had done an amazing job by carving all the little scales, mouth and even fire in the biscuit.

The fire!

"You made it breathe fire!" Michael shouted.

"Yea, I didn't know it was gonna come alive!"

The dragon saw them and breathed fire.

Michael jumped back.

The warmth slamming into him.

The Dragon roared.

The biscuits dogs and cats howled.

The dragon flapped its wing.

It flew.

It dived for Michael.

Thompson grabbed it.

The dragon attacked.

Spitting fire at him.

Thompson's arm caught light.

Michael rushed over.

Grabbed some water.

Throwing it at his boyfriend.

The dragon flew away.

It was out of the kitchen.

Michael went after it.

The dragon hovered round the tree.

It opened its mouth.

Michael couldn't let the tree be damaged.

He rushed over.

The dragon saw him.

Launching a fireball.

Michael dived out the way.

Hitting his head against the wall.

Pain flooded his head.

He sank to the floor.

The dragon knocked him over.

Thompson threw a biscuit dog at the dragon.

The dragon ate it.

Flying away.

As Thompson helped Michael get up, Michael

couldn't believe how crazy this Christmas was, all he wanted, needed was to spend it with the man he loved. Not get attacked by some crazy biscuit dragon.

The entire place stunk horribly of foul smoke and burnt biscuits, but he knew what he had to do. That foul dragon was stuck in the flat and now Michael got to live out one of his fantasies in a way, he had to defeat a dragon.

"Mich, ya okay?"

Michael ignored Thompson and focused on how to defeat a dragon made of biscuits, he didn't have too long before the dragon was bound to attack again, or at least eat one of the cute dogs and cats.

Then he got an idea, biscuits were useless after they were wet, but that was for normal biscuits. He wasn't sure if getting living biscuits wet would be enough.

He had to try. Michael was determined to have a perfect Christmas with his boyfriend, and that would hopefully all start when this dragon was dead.

"Got any spray bottles?" Michael asked.

Thompson's eyebrows rose so Michael told him the idea and he agreed.

When Thompson went to go and get the bottles and fill them, the dragon roared, flying at Michael.

Michael jumped back.

The dragon flashed its claws.

It wanted to kill Michael.

Michael felt his stomach turn.

The dragon spun around.

Unleashing torrents of fire at Michael.
He ducked.
The splashes of heat making him sweat.
The dragon charged.
Michael jumped.
The dragon turned at the last moment.
Catching Michael's shoulder.
Blood squirted out.
Michael screamed.
The dragon roared.
Launching fire.
It hit Michael.
The flames licked his flesh.
He fell to the ground.
Searing pain ripping through his body.
The dragon landed on his back.
Michael was shocked by the weight of it.
He couldn't breathe.
He tried to move.
He couldn't.
The dragon pressed its teeth into Michael's neck.
Michael screamed in agony.
Thompson threw something.
The dragon jumped.
Michael spun.
Kicking the dragon off him.
Thompson threw him a bottle.
Michael caught it.
The dragon flew at him.
Launching fire.

Michael sprayed.

The fire died.

Michael didn't stop.

He kept spraying.

It hit the dragon.

The dragon screamed.

Its mouth started to fall apart.

Michael and Thompson kept spraying.

The dragon fell to the ground.

Michael undid the lid.

Pouring the entire bottle onto the biscuit.

Thompson did the same.

Michael looked at the dragon as it melted away and Thompson scooped it up and burn it safely on the hob.

He went over to the sofa and allowed the softness to claim him, after everything that had happened the softness of the sofa felt even more amazing than normal. Michael had no intention of moving for the rest of the night.

Gently pressing where the dragon had bit into his neck Michael was surprised to see how there was barely a mark, blood or anything that suggested it was ever attacked. At the time it had felt like someone had stabbed him and ripped out his flesh, but his lack of injuries was hardly the weirdest thing of the night.

Michael just forgot about it. Glad to be alive unburned and able to enjoy Christmas.

When Thompson came out of the kitchen and pressed himself into Michael as they cuddled on the sofa, Michael couldn't believe how weird of a first Christmas this had been together.

Yet he still wouldn't have it any other way, it was fun, crazy and it showed how much Thompson loved him, and to Michael that meant everything. After years on the streets with an unloving family, he just wanted someone who could love him back.

And Thompson was definitely that man, and Michael just played with his beautiful hair as they cuddled on together, enjoying the rest of their first Christmas together.

"Wanna watch a fantasy film?"

Michael playfully hit him on the head as he didn't think he was going to be watching any film with a dragon or magic or anything else in for a little while. He had survived (with a few minor injuries) a dragon attack and as much as Michael loved those films, he didn't want to be reminded of the Biscuit Dragon for a long time to come.

Instead all he wanted was just to enjoy a weird First Christmas with Thompson with a cuddle, some Christmas music and maybe a little more later in the night.

INTRODUCTION
Mood/ Genre: Heart-warming Contemporary Fantasy

To continue with the fantasy section of this Extravaganza, we turn our attention to a certain aspect of Christmas and the holiday season that the vast majority of us thankfully never ever have had to experience.

And that is rejection.

Now please relax, the story itself is extremely heart-warming that is why I wrote the story, because I wanted to remind us all that Christmas is a magic time of year and amazing things can happen.

So this is why I choose this story to be the one that goes out on Christmas Eve, because there will sadly be people on Earth tonight that aren't spending time with loved ones, family and their friends.

Some people will be kicked out on the streets, abandoned and unloved by their families because of what they are, who they love and many more factors.

But if anything else, this story truly reminds us of the need, desire and utter magic that family provides us with. Not necessarily a blood family, but another much more precious kind.

So please expect a wonderfully heart-warming fantasy story about love, magic and what the true meaning of Christmas is all about.

Enjoy!

ALL FEAST

Ryan walked down the little path through the massive forest beside his amazing, wonderful boyfriend Tao, and he wouldn't have it any other way. The trees were massive thick pines filling the air with their sweet piney scents that Ryan really liked.

He wasn't sure why Tao was leading him through the forest on a path that was clearly never used on Christmas Eve. In his ideal world Ryan would have loved Tao to invite him round, spend the evening with him and hopefully roll around in a bed together.

But there was something about Tao that made Ryan sure he wasn't interested in taking their relationship to the next level yet. Ryan wished he would, but he was patient and he did love Tao, so he would wait.

The sound of birds, elves and phoenixes echoed around the forest as the sun started to set. Ryan liked the bitter coldness of winter, there was something pleasant about its bite. And if anything else, it might provide the perfect excuse for him to snuggle up next to Tao, wherever he was leading him.

From everything he had heard about the forest, Ryan really didn't know anything of interest up here, the forest was largely endless miles of trees and lakes and a few cabins sprinkled in from a bygone age, when humans thought it was right to hunt down the magical creatures that lived in these parts.

Ryan looked up at Tao as he continued to lead them on. Tao wore his normal tight blue jeans that left nothing to the imagination, his black hiking boots and a great black hoody.

And there was just something about Tao, maybe it was the way he walked, smiled and just projected confidence that Ryan loved so much about him.

When Ryan saw Tao look back at him and smile, he couldn't believe how great he felt. He was outside with the man he loved, going to a secret place for Christmas, hopefully. For Christmas Eve might have been about family traditionally but as his family had so plainly put it to him a few months ago, there was nothing traditional, right or sane about what Ryan loved.

They didn't care too much about family then. And Ryan didn't care too much either.

The smell of smoke made Ryan look up and he stopped when he saw a large stone mansion in the middle of a clearing. Ryan had heard of rich old people building great mansions in these parts of the woods decades ago, but he had always believed them to be just myths and legends.

But this mansion was stunning, Ryan hoped that this was where Tao was going to take him, the warm, ancient setting would be so romantic, so perfect and just what Ryan needed after a bad year.

Tao turned around. Ryan loved his smooth cheeks, stunning longish hair and that amazing smile that could melt even the toughest of hearts.

"Happy All Feast Beautiful," Tao said walking towards the mansion.

Ryan just stood there. The All Feast? He had never heard of such a thing, Tao had never mentioned it, Ryan didn't celebrate or know of it. What had he just walked into? Or perhaps the better question was, what had his boyfriend led him into?

After he walked through the front door, Ryan was stunned by the ancient wooden hallway and beautiful stone staircase that went up steeply and the canvas painting on the walls were impressive. This definitely was once home to a rich, spoiled person. No normal person could afford such things, at least not to as grand a scale.

The sound of two distinctive sets of footsteps that came out of the kitchen area at the end of the hallway, and Ryan was pleasantly surprised to see another two young, loved up men. Two friends of Tao.

Ryan had met Jim with his bright ginger hair and Francis a number of times over the past few months, from what he could tell they were Tao's best friends and they had been together since last Christmas when Jim's family had thrown him on the streets. Ryan wasn't sure why, it was either because he was gay or they were too poor to feed him, and him being gay was the perfect excuse to get rid of him.

But Ryan was a little surprised that he was really glad to see them. He liked them, they were both great people, and as sad as it sounded, any friend of Tao was a friend of his. Yet his entire body relaxed at the sight of them.

It was probably because Ryan had just wanted to be round people who respected his choices and weren't going to give him so much grief.

"Hi," Ryan said to both of them.

Jim and Francis both smiled at him. It wasn't a normal smile by any means, there was definitely something going on, Ryan just wanted to find out what.

"Tao, have you told him? Have you told him?" Jim said, his voice high pitched and excited.

Tao's fingers grazed Ryan's shoulder, Ryan savoured the feeling.

"Na, I thought we tell him later," Tao said, giving Jim and Francis a friendly hug.

Ryan had no idea what All Feast was, it was clearly something important to the three of them. Why didn't they just tell him? Ryan wanted, needed to know.

He almost started to feel left out, like back in school when the cool kids knew something great and the wannabes didn't.

"Beautiful?" Tao said.

Ryan quickly smiled and hoped Tao didn't think he was jealous or too desperate to learn the secret.

Jim walked back into the kitchen.

"So what's All Feast?" Ryan asked.

Francis smiled. "Ya'll find out soon enough,"

Jim came back holding a sort of sweatshirt. "Here, Put it on please,"

Jim threw the sweatshirt over to Ryan.

It was only then that Ryan looked at Jim and Francis and noticed that they were both wearing the exact same black sweatshirt with a Christmas pudding in the middle. Surely it was a couple thing.

But Tao gently rubbed Ryan's shoulder. "Please,"

Ryan always loved how velvety and beautiful Tao's voice was, so he could hardly refuse.

"Come on Laddie, ya can change upstairs if ya shy. I can explain something to ya too," Francis said, walking up the stone staircase.

Ryan followed.

As they walked into a wonderfully large bedroom with brown oak walls and a massive old bed into the middle fit for a king (or two in this case), Ryan felt the excitement build within him. He would love to spend the night (or forever) in a place like this. It would be amazing to pretend to be a king and actually have some power after the year he had had.

Ryan took off his shirt and started to put on the sweatshirt.

"So what is All Feast?" Ryan said, his voice a little more desperate than he wanted.

Francis laughed. "I did tell Tao to tell ya before ya came. It is great to have ya though. Jim's been wanting to have ya for months,"

"Have me for what?"

"For All Feast. Our version of Christmas,"

Ryan finished putting on the sweatshirt, realising it was a little tight and left nothing to the imagination, but at least Tao would see his slight muscles.

"Sorry. Wrong size. I'll remember for next year,"

Ryan was surprised at that. No one had ever fussed over him like that before, Ryan's entire life had been a case of if you don't like it, tough, be grateful you little so and so. Ryan bit back a small swell of emotion, he didn't want to feel so emotional but that simple sentence had meant so much to him.

"Ya know how Christmas is all about family, food and love?" Francis said.

Ryan nodded.

"Ma Family is good. Support, respect, love me. Don't really care if I'm there or not. Jim's fam, well, kicked him out and poor to the limit. Tossed him out the second they could,"

Ryan nodded and gestured Francis to stop. He really didn't want to hear what happened to Tao, he already knew. He hated Tao's family for what they did to him, all the hate, abuse and outrage aimed at him every hour of every day.

At least Ryan never had to meet them with Tao

cutting them out of his life.

"Yea, sorry I forgot ya two talk about it," Francis said. "And yours? Tao told us some,"

Ryan smiled. "My family. There's arguing, hate and no respect for my choices. I'm wrong, unnatural and deserve to have the gay beaten out of me with a big stick,"

Francis laughed hard at that. "The things peeps believe,"

Ryan smiled, truly smiled. Realising it was the first time he had smiled in a long, long time with anyone else but Tao. It felt good, it felt great, it felt right.

"All Feast?" Ryan asked.

"Oh yea, none of us have love, food and family. So made our own, there's no religion, no hate, no nothing. The three of us have to agree on everything, no one can come unless we want to and everything is done together,"

Ryan took a step back. That all sounded strangely wonderful, a Christmas or Christmas time without any arguing about the decorations, lights or anything else. Christmas could be what it was meant to be about, loving your family.

Family didn't have to be blood and that was what Ryan loved about gays, because it was like one big family. Especially with his wonderful, beautiful Tao and his two friends.

Ryan just felt at home here, there was something so peaceful, comfortable and even magical about the entire thing. At last after a rough start to his life and everything that happened a few months ago, he could finally start to live life how he wanted and loved who he wanted without any negatives.

It felt like a massive weight had just lifted and Ryan couldn't wait to celebrate All Feast with his new forged family.

"So ya know All Feast is what it meant to be. A Feast for All no matter who or what ya are, ya are always welcome here. And Tao begged me to let ya come. I was always going to say yes, but it was funny seeing him beg,"

Ryan felt another wave of emotion flood him, he had never known Tao to show that much emotion about him. Ryan wasn't sure if Tao was even really into him anymore, he hadn't been as emotional, passionate or loving towards him lately.

But maybe Ryan was wrong. He hoped so, so badly.

"Come on Laddie, gonna make more foods for the Feast. Tao didn't tell me what ya wanted for the Feast, so…"

It was silly that Ryan was so shocked, but to him, he had never been asked these questions. No one had ever cared about him this much before. He had always been given things and forced to enjoy them, it never mattered what he wanted.

But it did here.

"Biscuits?" Ryan forced out.

Francis cocked his head. "Biscuits? I… oh Jim

likes them too. Ginger nut okay,"

Gays, nuts and… Ryan really tried hard not to make a joke. But everyone was family here, so Ryan knew he had to start relaxing and unlearning all the things he had taught himself over the years. Because he had to act straight, he had to be a certain way.

But now… now he could be himself.

Yet the joke moment had definitely passed now anyway.

"Yea ginger nuts are great," Ryan said.

Francis smiled. "You're telling me,"

After they went back downstairs and into the kitchen, Francis gestured to Jim to come with him and Ryan went into the kitchen.

The house might have been old but the kitchen was stunning. Ryan had always had a soft spot for "real" kitchens with a massive kitchen island in the middle with a large oven, plenty of brown cupboards and most importantly Tao standing at the island mixing a bowl.

Ryan went up behind him, wrapped his arms around Tao and rested his head on Tao's strong shoulders.

"Thank you for this," Ryan said, kissing Tao's neck. "Who's house is this?"

Ryan saw Tao smile. "Ya welcome. It's mine now. My fam signed it over to me as a peace offering months ago. It didn't work but I, we, have a house,"

Ryan ignored the *we* part, that would get him way too emotional. That was for sure.

"What you making?" Ryan asked.

"You always said you liked ginger nuts at Christmas,"

Ryan couldn't speak as he just let his stomach tense and relax. Tao was amazing that was for sure.

"No one has ever done this for me before. Why you doing it?" Ryan asked.

Tao spun around and wrapped his own arms around Ryan.

"Because you're important to me. I want you to become part of my life and my family,"

Ryan felt his eyes wet at the sound of someone actually wanting him.

"Live with me. Be with me. Love with me," Tao said, grazing Ryan's lips.

"Done," Ryan said, kissing him.

And as Tao sadly broke the kiss and turned back to mixing up the mixture in the bowl, Ryan just stood there for a moment, savouring the feel of Tao against him.

This really was going to be the start of an amazing new life with people who actually loved with and wanted him around. That feeling would definitely take time to get used to but Ryan didn't mind in the slightest.

Ryan ran his hands up Tao before he broke away and grabbed a mixing bowl of his own, and stared at the stunning man who he was hopefully, happily going to spend the rest of his life with.

It didn't matter what happened in his life now,

Ryan had his family, an amazing boyfriend and soon a wonderful All Feast that was going to be the first of many more to come.

INTRODUCTION

Mood/ Genre: Light(ish) contemporary fantasy

For the penultimate fantasy short story of the Extravaganza, I really wanted to explore a fantasy concept that has increased in popularity in recent years.

For so long, time has been believed to be a straight line or a timestream of some sort that could or couldn't be manipulated. But over the course of the past year and a bit the concept of time as a wheel has become very popular. From the amazing *Wheel of Time* TV series on Prime Video (and the books is based on) to The Amazing Mr Blunden.

As well as I must confess that this short story was written after me and my family watched the 2021 remake of The Amazing Mr Blunden because I wanted to explore this concept even more. And as always I do this concept in my own characteristically… darker and slightly more interesting way compared to the children's movie that inspired it.

Therefore, definitely read on or download the next Extravaganza story about family, loss and most importantly The Wheel of Years.

You'll love this one!

WHEEL OF YEARS

Michael Smoff normally avoided cemeteries, but this was not a normal time. It was far from in fact. As the massive oak trees loomed over him like evil guardians of the dead, Michael ignored them as they blew in the wind and focused on the large headstone in front of him.

He never had liked cemeteries. They were awful things, always overused in horror films and filled with the dead. No one should ever have to go to them, Michael couldn't remember the last time he had been to one.

It could have been when his mother died a fierce hero saving thousands about a decade ago, but he couldn't remember. After everything he had been through he had avoided, pain, suffering and death as much as he could.

It was probably why he joined the Magic Healers Core straight out of university, so he could help others avoid what he couldn't. As much as he loved those times fighting with the British Army all over the world, he still saw more friends die than he would wish on anyone else.

But the Wheel of Years kept turning.

The Wheel was such a stupid idea. Most ideas that Magical and definitely non-magical people had were plain stupid. Michael never ever understood the so-called greatness about the Wheel.

The entire silly idea was about time, and by extension years, went round and round and round on a wheel and everyone was at different points on the same wheel all turning, living and breathing.

On paper it was a brilliant idea to Michael. He loved the theoretical concept of it. But in practice, why the hell did the Wheel keep turning?

As much as he hated the pointless non-magical religions (Magical peeps didn't have religions as far as Michael remembered), at least those religions gave their worshippers a sense that the turn of their Wheel was by designed.

By in magical lore, the Wheel of Years kept turning, no matter how many people were mindlessly killed, starved and slaughtered.

It made no sense to Michael whatsoever, he wanted to change it, he wanted to fix it, he wanted to break the Wheel.

The foul smell of horrible damp, ash and rot of the cemetery reminded Michael that he should never think like that. He had seen too many great magic users fall to the Darkness this year alone because they had wanted to break the Wheel. Yet if the Wheel stopped turning then chaos was unleashed and the Darkness ruled over the disorder.

Michael never believed such craziness growing up but this year... the Darkness had been growing stronger and stronger and stronger. It seemed to know exactly where to attack the NATO, British and American forces. It seemed to know everything. The Darkness was growing bolder, infecting everyone and everything it could to stop the Magic Core from living in peace.

The sound of the cold howling wind made Michael focus on the headstone again. It was disgusting but he didn't expect anything less from a Follower of the Darkness, with its black stone surface that looked to be covered in mould. Even the trees, bushes and flowers around the headstone had been morphed into a nightmarish reality.

Nothing around the headstone looked natural or pleasant.

The entire scene was outrageous to Michael, this was the disgraceful reality the world would fall into if the Darkness grew.

Then Michael noticed how the trees, bushes and flowers seem to turn and focus on him. He didn't want to be here but he had a purpose, he had to witness the Wheel for himself, or at the very least he had to think about the New Year.

Michael had never understood why his brother (the owner of the Headstone) had fallen to the

Darkness this year. His Tour with a Scottish Regiment had been great until his brother turned. The Scottish were always great people with their rich folklore, sense of humour and amazing food.

But Michael despised how his brother hated the Scottish and went out of his way to make them seem like fools. It was about that time Michael should have known his brother was falling to the Darkness, listening to its whispers and enjoying its touch.

By the time Michael realised, it was far too late. Michael tried to reason with him, tried to save him, tried to help him. His brother wasn't listening, so they fought and the brother died.

Just looking at the disgusting headstone made Michael want to walk away and forget about his brother and his mistakes. But the New Year would be upon him in a few days and then the Wheel would have turned again.

Michael had to talk to his brother, for better or for worse. He shouldn't have wanted to do it, it was probably against magical law, but the greatest thing about death and stepping away from the Wheel, was his brother could be stripped of the Darkness. Meaning his brother might be his true self if he did this magical trick.

Michael had to take the chance.

He extended his hand towards the gravestone, thought about his brother and watched as rays of white light came out.

"Return to me brother for a little time, a little

turn, a little... sibling love," Michael said.

The headstone hummed a little as the half-blown off face of a young man popped out of the headstone and his smashed up arms pulled the rest of him out of the headstone.

Michael wasn't sure of his brother's appearance. He made sure he couldn't remember his brother's name as names had power. And if his brother had truly, truly fallen to the Darkness then saying his name could resurrect him to full life (and not this mere shadow of life that Michael had gifted him).

Michael could never allow his brother to return to the Darkness' service.

When his brother stood up, Michael shook his head at the disgusting twisted form of his brother. His body was normally tall, slim and attractive, having plenty of women chasing after him. No one would chase after him now.

His brother gave Michael a twisted smile. "You call Michael. Do you want to embrace the Darkness? It's erotic touch. You must Michael,"

Michael couldn't believe what he was hearing. This wasn't his brother. His brother was softly spoken, he would never use the word *erotic* or anything so... forward. Michael hated to imagine what else the Darkness had done to him.

"What you seen the Wheel?" Michael asked.

His brother spat on the headstone. "The Wheel! The Wheel is foul. It must be destroyed. The Wheel turns and turns and turns. Singing to itself! Whilst I died. It turns and does nothing whilst we suffer!"

Michael just wanted to return his brother (or whatever this thing was) but he had to get answers. He didn't know what answers he needed, Michael realised he had wanted them to questions he didn't know. He supposed he just wanted to know more about the Wheel and what he needed to do in the New Year to keep everyone he loved safe.

"We all suffer Brother. I mourned your loss. I didn't want to kill you,"

"And the Wheel just turned,"

Michael shook his head. "The Wheel cannot be destroyed. The Darkness cannot be allowed to rule. You have seen what it does,"

"No Michael. It is you that cannot be allowed to rule. You know nothing of its touch. It is freeing,"

Michael took a step back.

"The Darkness allows me to see the Wheel turning, hear its gear and everyone who makes it up,"

Michael smiled. He was getting somewhere. "What do you mean everyone who makes it up?"

His Brother stepped towards him. "The Wheel will always turn. The Wheel is made up of everyone. Everyone is a gear in the turning of the Wheel. The only way to break the Wheel is to break everyone and recast their souls in the Darkness,"

Michael couldn't completely understand what his brother was saying, so he was saying that everyone on Earth was a part of the Wheel in one way or another. Meaning he was too. That was good, very good. If

Michael could find out more about each so-called gear. Then maybe he could figure out how to help the... other gears move against the Darkness?

"Tell me Michael, the Wheel keeps turning, you keep suffering, you keep losing. Why do you fight and turn with the Wheel?"

Michael didn't actually know. He had always fought against the Darkness since he had been a teenager, it was what his parents had done and he had joined the army to stop the Darkness from growing. But he had never asked himself why, and he wasn't going to start now.

"Can you see me in the Wheel?" Michael asked.

His brother smiled. "Of course. The Darkness lets me see all. Should I tell you the Wheel's reading?"

"You can lie. Twist the truth. Bend Reality. I will not be fooled so easily,"

"Michael, mother and father saw the Wheel once before they died. The Darkness granted them a gift,"

Michael wasn't having this. His mother and father were heroes, his mother had died to save thousands. They hadn't fallen to the Darkness, they wouldn't, they couldn't!

"It is truth Michael. Mother and Father were dying. The Darkness offered them a gift. They saw the Wheel then the Darkness killed them anyway. It was what they deserved,"

"How can you say that!"

"Our parents were deniers of the Darkness. They had to die!"

"They loved you,"

"I never loved them. The Darkness is my family,"

Michael shot out his hand. White light shot out. His Brother hissed in pain.

"Tell me what the Wheel says about me,"

His Brother chuckled and closed his eyes. "The Darkness focuses on Russia, China and America. The Alliances of old are undone. The Darkness causes a new World War, a war that eclipses the other two,"

Michael truly hated his brother. He extended his hand out more. His brother hissed loudly.

"The Wheel turns you one option. You fight, save Russia but die in the process. The Wheel keeps turning, correcting and Darkness grows again and completes its mission. World War Three starts as the Wheel turns once more,"

Michael smiled.

"What are you smiling at!" his Brother shouted.

Michael realised in that moment that his Brother had told him two vital things. The first was hardly a surprise, it was clear as day his brother was lying. The Darkness was powerful but it was delusion plain and simple. Michael had met with hundreds of Darkness infected people and every single one spoke about the same delusion. The Great Infection of Russia, China and America.

All three superpowers were infected and the world would fall.

Michael had heard that same delusion for twenty

years now. Every Infected person saying it would happen on the next Turning of the Wheel, but it hadn't in the past twenty years.

His brother had truly fallen to the Darkness, but that wasn't what Michael was interested in, at least not really.

He realised how powerful the Wheel truly was, he had heard once how the Wheel and Darkness were a constant storm against each other. Each one fighting to either maintain or annihilate Order, but Michael had forgotten a simple saying about the true power of the Wheel.

The Wheel had the power to correct itself when the Darkness won, and that was what Michael had to do. He had to keep fighting the Darkness, protecting the Wheel and letting it turn so all the innocent people could live in some kind of order in this chaotic world.

Michael looked at his brother. "You really have fallen Brother,"

"Say my name. I know you know it. Say my name,"

"Goodbye Brother. I return you to death and let the Darkness have you," Michael said coldly.

His brother screamed in agony as the headstone sucked him back in.

Then the world was silent, the wind did not howl or blow and the entire cemetery was just as cold and creepy as it had been when Michael first walked in.

As Michael walked away from the headstone, his

mission or purpose for the New Year was clear. He had to keep fighting the Darkness, keep the Wheel turning and just hope that the delusion of the Darkness would never come.

World War Three and the Great Infection could never come to part, but Michael looked forward to the Darkness trying. He loved a challenge and whenever the Wheel turned it meant he had done his job well for another year.

And that is what he wanted. Protecting the innocent, keeping the Darkness at bay and enjoying life, now that was what kept Michael alive, and he loved it.

As he left the cemetery, Michael was determined to keep the Wheel of Years turning for years to come.

FANTASTICAL CHRISTMAS COMPLETE COLLECTION

INTRODUCTION
Mood/ Genre: Dark Fantasy

As one of the last fantasy short stories in the Holiday Extravaganza, it turned out I wanted to write something rather dark and twisted and harsh. Since my muse decided that it didn't want to write anything more positive to end the fantasy section of the Extravaganza on.

But in a way this is actually perfect in the long run because it will soon be new year, a time for celebration, continued happiness and new beginnings. And it turned out my muse had a very different way to interpret this meaning of the New year.

Whilst I don't think my muse wants this to be a new series, I could definitely see how it could be expanded out into books and novellas and other short stories.

But we will see if my muse wants any of that in the future.

In the meantime, I would highly, highly

recommend you make yourself a very large and nice mug of hot chocolate or coffee (or both in my case) and prepare yourself for this dark tale about magic, extremism and love.

Enjoy!

REPENT

"Repent For Tomorrow You Die,"

That is exactly what Wizard Novice Garry Mitchel heard three times an hour as he sat alone chained to his metal chair in his freezing cold interrogation room with its metal black walls, single candle that dripped wax onto the ground as it badly illumined the room and the large metal door just stared at him.

It might have been nearing Christmas, or maybe it was new year, for so many people but Garry would be honestly surprised if he even made it to New year.

When him and his friends had been attacked, Garry tried to fight back. He tried to unleash torrents of flame from his hands, he tried to teleport away, he tried to do anything.

But he couldn't.

Garry hated the disgusting smell of cigar smoke that filtered through the metal door. It was the exact horrific smell that filled his leader's house before the monstrous men attacked. And it still left the same horrible taste of his friends' blood on his tongue as it did during the attack.

Garry just wanted to be with his fellow wizards and witches. He wanted to laugh, have fun and get to know how to use his powers for good. It had already helped his family save on their energy bills by heating and cooking their meals using his magic.

That was just the most recent way he had used his powers for good.

But clearly just because he was different, he was a monster to some people. Garry had laughed in the face of his attackers when they accused him of killing people, burning animals alive and plotting to enslave the world.

Garry would never do such a thing. Neither would any of his friends.

Yet of course extremists can never see reason. Garry's ribs still ached from the constant beating, lashing of chains and punches that the attackers gave him daily. They had even cut off his toes and a foot on Christmas Day (Garry wasn't sure what the days were anymore) as a so-called *special Christmas treat*.

Garry just wanted to go home to his family, hug them and make sure they were okay. But Garry didn't know where here was, he could still be in the South East of England, or he could be in the North or overseas.

He just didn't know.

Instead of sleeping he tried every single night like

clockwork to practice his magic. All he needed was to conjure up some kind of flame, energy or something to break free and hopefully kill his attackers.

Garry didn't want to kill them. Him and his friends hated violence of any sort but Garry had to be free. He knew these attackers were never going to stop interrogating and torturing him.

The attackers were implying that there was some kind of grand Magical resistance group that was plotting to destroy the United Kingdom and burn it to the ground.

Garry had no doubt there were some craziness like that, but were they just as many (and probably more) of non-magic crazies?

The sound of harsh wild voices came from the other side of the metal door. Garry felt his heart race but he managed to force himself to relax and calm down, getting fearful wasn't going to save him.

He just had to survive, escape and warn the very few magic friends he had left about this group of crazies.

"Repent for tomorrow you die,"

Garry bit his lip as the metal door opened, unleashing a massive blast of icy cold air and two men walked in.

If Garry had met these men on the street then he probably would have given them a second look at the very least. They were both very tall, slim and fit in a rather attractive way. Garry liked how they both seemed perfectly normal by their looks, but Garry hated them.

These two were monsters.

Garry just forced himself to look into their cold, dark eyes and he saw no sense of humanity, warmth or love in them. He had no idea how these two men went wrong but something did. And it had produced the most monstrous people Garry had ever met.

Garry tried to shoot out his hand despite the tight metal chains wrapped round them. He willed his hand to shoot out fire.

Nothing happened.

The two men kicked him in the stomach.

Pain ripped through Garry. He screamed in agony.

"Repent!" the two men shouted whacking Garry with two necklaces with the Holy Cross on them.

That was just Garry's luck. Because an ancient book said magic was the devil's work, he was now being tortured, doomed to death and punished for something that wasn't his fault.

As much as Garry knew that the vast majority of all religions, including Islam and Christianity, were perfectly peaceful, loving religions. Garry still hated the extremists.

The tallest of the two wrapped his hands round Garry's throat.

"You must Repent for what you are. You must ask Him for forgiveness. You must help us destroy the rest of you," he said.

Garry would love to know what he had been

drinking or smoking or snorting up his nose, but sadly Garry just knew this idiot was being serious.

"What have my people done to you?" Garry asked.

The two men laughed.

"This is not about what you *have* done. It is about what you *will* do to us all. It is only a matter of time," they both said.

Garry really couldn't understand the logic between these idiots. Witches and wizards had done nothing to them, but for some reason these men were so scared of magic that they were willing to torture and kill him over Christmas.

It made no sense.

"One last chance," the shortest man said. "Repent before Him and tell us where your network is,"

Garry just shook his head. He wasn't going to apologise for being who he was and using his powers for good.

He had no reason to apologise.

And there was no chance in hell, Garry was going to send his friends to the same fate as him.

"We have to kill him then," the tallest man said.

"By His will and to kill a heretic," the shortest man said.

Yep. These two men were definitely extremists.

They both whipped out knives.

Garry tried to shoot out his hand.

No flame came out.

No magic came out.

Nothing happened.

Garry willed his magic to do something.

It wasn't working.

The men thrusted the knives into his stomach.

As the sheer shock and horror ripped through Garry, he really wished he wasn't such a pathetic wizard. He had to escape and do something.

Someone knocked on the door.

The two men opened it just enough for them two to talk to the person on the other side, but Garry couldn't see who they were talking to.

He heard the scary conversation though. To his utter horror.

"Three witches found two miles outside. Our people have captured them. They killed four wizards too," the person on the other side said.

"Excellent," the tallest man said.

"They are being transported here as we speak," the man on the other side said.

The shortest man smiled and looked back at Garry.

"Then we kill them all," he said.

Garry wanted to scream, lash out and kill them all. But he was far too weak to do that.

As the idiots continued talking Garry had to focus, that was apparently one of the most important lessons when it came to using magic.

Apparently magic was all about focus, power, effect.

Garry had to focus on making magical flame shoot out of his hands. He couldn't let innocent people die or suffer or be tortured because of his weakness.

He felt something inside him click into place.

Garry closed his eyes and willed his emotion, love and hate for these monsters to power his healing and his magic.

Garry felt something akin to a fire burn away inside of him.

The monsters ripped the knives out of him.

But no blood came out of Garry's body as he felt utter uncontrolled magic pour into every single fibre of his being.

He forced his skin and muscle and flesh to remould itself and repair his body.

Garry opened his eyes to see the two monsters dive at him. Their knives wanting to rip into his body. But with a single thought the knives turned to ash and the two men simply fell into Garry.

They knocked the chair over.

Garry's head hit the floor.

But he didn't care.

For he was dealing with the stupidity of mortals who feared him for no reason. He could kill them so easily now, he could melt their minds or make them kill each other.

He didn't know how he knew that, he just did.

But Garry was not a monster.

"Apologise to me. Quit your evil ways. Repent to

me," Garry said.

The two men jumped up.

They went to stomp on Garry.

Garry rolled his eyes and the two men screamed in crippling agony as they were boiled inside out.

When the two corpses dropped to the ground with a thud, Garry was surprised at everything that was going on. When he was with his friends he was never this powerful.

But Garry had always had more emotion, love and hate within than any of the others. And Garry realised that emotion was the true root of magic and power, so in a way it made sense for him to be powerful.

If he ever had to explain it to anyone he would explain it as if magic was a fire, he had the most petrol to throw on top.

"Masters?" a young man said, walking in with a machine gun.

He saw the two bodies and stared at Garry. The young man was so fearful but Garry really didn't want to kill him.

"Free me," Garry commanded. "I do not want to hurt you,"

The young man raised his machine gun.

"Die unholy abomination!"

The young man clicked the trigger. Bullets shot out.

Garry rolled his eyes.

The bullets just froze in the air and ripped

through the young man.

Garry hated himself for having to do it. But it was the only way. He had to believe that.

It was him or Garry.

Knowing that those innocent young witches would turn up in chains and die at any moment Garry waved his restricted hand and all the chains fell away from him.

He had to save those girls.

Garry jumped up and raced out of the interrogation room.

Garry was immediately greeted by a long metal corridor with large windows showing they were on a cold ground floor of an abandoned building in the middle of the woods with endless sheets of snow covering the trees and ground.

The sound of crying, shouting and shrieking echoed into the long corridor from the tiny metal door at the other end.

Slowly Garry walked along the corridor, not knowing what to expect. He didn't know if these people would have more troops, more weapons, more anything.

After half a minute of walking down the corridor, Garry carefully opened the metal door and peeked into wherever those sounds were coming from.

Garry was shocked at the horrific sight of a small garage, probably meant for food deliveries and what not, with its large grey cargo bay, concrete ceiling and solid metal door.

Now a small lorry was docked and two women wearing black uniforms were dragging out six teenage girls on the verge of turning 18. A very dangerous age for magic users as that was the age when their power really developed.

Another five black uniformed women, each carrying a pistol, met the group and smiled like predators do when they have their prey right where they want them.

Garry didn't want anyone to suffer or die tonight. He had to at least try to convince some of them to surrender and abandon this murderous path.

He just had to try.

"Please stop," Garry said as he marched into the garage.

All the seven women had their pistols trained on him.

"You don't have to kill them. They have done nothing wrong," Garry said.

"They are unholy creatures. They have been touched by the devil. Christ was born two thousand years ago, it is our job to complete his work!" one of them shouted.

Garry literally had no reply for that crazy talk. Garry didn't care what himself, these people or anyone believed, but if Jesus was real then surely he wouldn't have wanted the murder of innocent girls?

All the women's pistols shot out laser targets onto Garry's chests.

He looked at those poor innocent little girls.

They looked so fearful, sweaty and like they just wanted to go home and celebrate with their families.

Garry didn't even know if he had a family anymore. These people probably tracked down his family, friends and killed them all.

In fact.

Garry focused on those girls more and more and he recognised each and every one of them. They were known to his friends, they were known to the magic community, they would have been easy targets to pick up if anyone knew the magic folks in the area.

As much as Garry loved the celebrations, parties and the sense of community he got from the magic, well, community. He just knew it made them easy targets for those hunting them.

"Kill them all!" a woman shouted.

The bullets screamed through the air.

Garry rolled his eyes.

The women dropped dead. Their dark red blood pouring out onto the cold garage floor.

Garry slowly walked over to the six teenage girls and they ran over to him and hugged him.

In all honesty, Garry might not have been many years older than them, but he was going to protect them. For a new age was dawning, the age where magical people had to go into hiding and it was no longer safe to remain in the light.

There were so many shadows all over the world for his people to hide in, but Garry didn't want to strictly hide.

Of course, he would tell his other wizards and witches the dangers and help them to hide, but he wasn't going to himself. If this torture and adventure had taught him anything, it was that he had to use his all emotion and love and powers for good no matter how dangerous the risk.

Garry was going to leave here (wherever here was) a changed man. A man that would protect everyone, find these girls a good home with other witches and wizards, and then Garry was going to do something that would protect everyone from a far.

He would hunt down these extremist groups, give them a chance to Repent and if they didn't, he would kill them.

Because at the end of the day, it truly was the extremists or the magic folk.

A choice Garry never ever wanted to make, but the world had forced him to do this.

So as he walked out of the cold abandoned building with his arms tightly round the girls who would protect him as much as he would them. Garry was looking forward to the new year, because everything was changing.

And that just made Garry really, really excited.

GET YOUR FREE AND EXCLUSIVE SHORT STORY NOW! LEARN ABOUT NEMESIO'S PAST!

https://www.subscribepage.com/fireheart

FANTASTICAL CHRISTMAS COMPLETE COLLECTION

About the author:

Connor Whiteley is the author of over 60 books in the sci-fi fantasy, nonfiction psychology and books for writer's genre and he is a Human Branding Speaker and Consultant.

He is a passionate warhammer 40,000 reader, psychology student and author.

Who narrates his own audiobooks and he hosts The Psychology World Podcast.

All whilst studying Psychology at the University of Kent, England.

Also, he was a former Explorer Scout where he gave a speech to the Maltese President in August 2018 and he attended Prince Charles' 70th Birthday Party at Buckingham Palace in May 2018.

Plus, he is a self-confessed coffee lover!

More From The Holiday Extravaganza:

Criminal Christmas:

Crime, Christmas, Closet
Protecting Christmas
Christmas Thief
Christmas, Crime, letter
Private Eye, Convention and Christmas
Cheater At Dinner
Perfect Christmas
Salvation In The Maid
Criminal, Resistance, Alliance
Dark Farm
Great Give Away

Sweet Christmas

Lights, Love, Christmas
Journalist, Zookeeper, Love
Young Romantic Hearts
Love In The Newspaper
Holiday, Burnout, Love
Homeless, Charity, Love
Cold December Night
Driving Home For Love
Love At The Winter Wedding
Fireworks, New Year, Love
Loving In The New Year Tourist

FANTASTICAL CHRISTMAS COMPLETE COLLECTION

<u>Fantastical Christmas:</u>
Magic That Binds
One Final Christmas
Author's Christmas Problems
Last Winter Dragon Egg
A Sacrifice For Saturnalia
Soulcaster
Weird First Christmas
All Feast
Solstice Guardian
Wheel of Years
Repent

OTHER SHORT STORIES BY CONNOR WHITELEY

<u>Mystery Short Stories:</u>

Poison In The Candy Cane

Christmas Innocence

You Better Watch Out

Christmas Theft

Trouble In Christmas

Smell of The Lake

Problem In A Car

Theft, Past and Team

Embezzler In The Room

A Strange Way To Go

A Horrible Way To Go

Ann Awful Way To Go

An Old Way To Go

A Fishy Way To Go

A Pointy Way To Go

A High Way To Go

A Fiery Way To Go

A Glassy Way To Go

A Chocolatey Way To Go

Kendra Detective Mystery Collection Volume 1

Kendra Detective Mystery Collection Volume 2

Stealing A Chance At Freedom

FANTASTICAL CHRISTMAS COMPLETE COLLECTION

Glassblowing and Death
Theft of Independence
Cookie Thief
Marble Thief
Book Thief
Art Thief
Mated At The Morgue
The Big Five Whoopee Moments
Stealing An Election
Mystery Short Story Collection Volume 1
Mystery Short Story Collection Volume 2

<u>Science Fiction Short Stories:</u>
The First Rememberer
Life of A Rememberer
System of Wonder
Lifesaver
Remarkable Way She Died
The Interrogation of Annabella Stormic
Blade of The Emperor
Arbiter's Truth
Computation of Battle
Old One's Wrath
Puppets and Masters
Ship of Plague
Interrogation
Edge of Failure

One Way Choice
Acceptable Losses
Balance of Power
Good Idea At The Time
Escape Plan
Escape In The Hesitation
Inspiration In Need
Singing Warriors
Knowledge is Power
Killer of Polluters
Climate of Death
The Family Mailing Affair
Defining Criminality
The Martian Affair
A Cheating Affair
The Little Café Affair
Mountain of Death
Prisoner's Fight
Claws of Death
Bitter Air
Honey Hunt
Blade On A Train

FANTASTICAL CHRISTMAS COMPLETE COLLECTION

<u>Fantasy Short Stories:</u>
City of Snow
City of Light
City of Vengeance
Dragons, Goats and Kingdom
Smog The Pathetic Dragon
Don't Go In The Shed
The Tomato Saver
The Remarkable Way She Died
The Bloodied Rose
Asmodia's Wrath
Heart of A Killer
Emissary of Blood
Dragon Coins
Dragon Tea
Dragon Rider
Sacrifice of the Soul
Heart of The Flesheater
Heart of The Regent
Heart of The Standing
Feline of The Lost
Heart of The Story
City of Fire
Awaiting Death

Other books by Connor Whiteley:

Bettie English Private Eye Series
A Very Private Woman
The Russian Case
A Very Urgent Matter
A Case Most Personal
Trains, Scots and Private Eyes
The Federation Protects

The Fireheart Fantasy Series
Heart of Fire
Heart of Lies
Heart of Prophecy
Heart of Bones
Heart of Fate

City of Assassins (Urban Fantasy)
City of Death
City of Marytrs
City of Pleasure
City of Power

Agents of The Emperor
Return of The Ancient Ones
Vigilance
Angels of Fire
Kingmaker

FANTASTICAL CHRISTMAS COMPLETE COLLECTION

<u>The Garro Series- Fantasy/Sci-fi</u>
GARRO: GALAXY'S END
GARRO: RISE OF THE ORDER
GARRO: END TIMES
GARRO: SHORT STORIES
GARRO: COLLECTION
GARRO: HERESY
GARRO: FAITHLESS
GARRO: DESTROYER OF WORLDS
GARRO: COLLECTIONS BOOK 4-6
GARRO: MISTRESS OF BLOOD
GARRO: BEACON OF HOPE
GARRO: END OF DAYS

<u>Winter Series- Fantasy Trilogy Books</u>
WINTER'S COMING
WINTER'S HUNT
WINTER'S REVENGE
WINTER'S DISSENSION

<u>Miscellaneous:</u>
RETURN
FREEDOM
SALVATION
Reflection of Mount Flame
The Masked One
The Great Deer

www.ingramcontent.com/pod-product-compliance
Lightning Source LLC
LaVergne TN
LVHW011834060526
838200LV00053B/4014